KRISTY'S
PUZZLE

RAWLINS Book 5

DEBORAH WALLACE

Deborah Wallace

Kristy's Puzzle: Rawlins Book 5

Published by Deborah Wallace

Copyright © 2020 by Deborah Wallace
5/23

ISBN: 978-1-951457-08-2

Cover Art by Raymond and Deborah Wallace
Rawlins town photo by Raymond Wallace

Chapter 1

Kristy Collins stood on her best friend's doorstep. The house was bigger than she expected, but nowhere near as big as Shauna's in-laws' house. Kristy had never thought much of children before, never even held a baby, but here she was in Rawlins—ready to wade into baby cries and dirty diapers for two weeks.

The door opened, and she held in a laugh at the tired and disheveled father. It wasn't a good image for the sexy guy. "Jason. Looks like you can use some help."

A yawn stretched his face, and he ran a hand through his dark hair—apparently not the first time. Blue, bloodshot eyes took her in. "I'm glad to see you, Kristy. Mom left two days ago. I don't know how a seven-pound kid can be so exhausting."

"Is that food on your shirt?"

He glanced at his shoulder. "The baby spit up on me. I'll change before I leave for work."

She grabbed her suitcase. "Well, let me see him. I'm anxious to meet my godson." She couldn't believe she'd agreed to take on a kid if something were to happen to Shauna and Jason. Of course, nothing would. As Shauna's bodyguard, Jason had saved her once, and he'd make sure nothing happened to her or his son.

He stretched out his hand. "Let me take your suitcase

upstairs, and you can visit with Shauna. She's in the living room." He took the case and the bag from her shoulder, then stepped back. "We're giving you the first room on the right. As far as you can get from the baby at night."

Kristy laughed. "I bet you wish you were."

He grinned. "I'm not admitting to anything."

As he headed toward the stairs, Kristy peeked into the kitchen. Shauna's normally spotless counters were littered with dishes. She'd fill the dishwasher the first chance she got.

She paused in the doorway to the living room. Shauna held little, dark-haired Logan. Her face glowed with the same love as when she gazed at her husband. The same way Jason stared at Shauna.

Kristy's heart lurched. She'd always enjoyed men, but had run before a serious relationship developed. The only role models she had were her parents, and she didn't want that.

Shauna glanced up and grinned. "Kristy! Come sit down. Wow. Look at your hair. It hasn't been that long since the beginning of high school."

Kristy shrugged. "New outlook, new hair. I've always liked it longer." She just didn't like guys pulling on it, and since there were no guys, she could do what she wanted.

Shauna ran a finger over her son's cheek. "He's almost done eating. Then you can hold him."

She'd come to take care of Shauna—prepare meals, do laundry, and fetch tea. She imagined herself on the periphery, watching Shauna and Jason hold Logan. She'd never touched a baby in her life, but since she was a godmother, she should get used to touching the kid.

She plopped down beside her friend, leaned against her, and tipped her head onto Shauna's shoulder for a moment. "I'm so happy for you. Who would have thought that celibate Shauna would be married with a baby?"

Shauna's face reddened. "Hey, I was just waiting for the right guy."

Kristy grinned. "Yeah. Man of your dreams. Literally." Shauna never told her specifics, just that she'd had steamy sex dreams with a guy named Jason. When Shauna had overheard her then fiancé ordering someone to be killed, she'd left her engagement ring behind and run to Kristy. Kristy's father hired the real Jason as Shauna's bodyguard, and he'd taken her to Rawlins to hide.

Kristy remembered the moment they met, and Shauna's fear when the man turned out to be real. But all Kristy could do was stare at the man who was with him. Mark. She'd had two wonderful months with him before she left. The worst mistake of her life, but she didn't know it at the time. Seventeen months, and she still regretted it.

Shauna put Logan on her shoulder and patted his back. After a moment, a small burp erupted from him, and she held the baby out to Kristy.

"Um. I might drop him. How about if I just touch him first?" She ran a finger over his cheek—the softest skin she'd ever felt.

Shauna nudged the little guy closer. "You're sitting down. And you won't drop him. Hold your arms out."

Still wary, Kristy accepted the precious bundle, her arms automatically wrapping around him.

"Make sure you always support his head."

She met Shauna's gaze with fear. "You mean if I'm not careful, I could break his neck?"

Shauna giggled. "I've never heard of it happening. It's just what everybody says. Maybe it makes their necks sore."

The little guy was warm, and she snuggled him closer. His eyebrows belonged to her best friend, but all the other features seemed pudgy. She had no idea how it could be, but he was adorable. He opened his blue eyes and stared at her.

She was a goner. In seconds, her godson had become family.

Her eyes widened. "He's…he's…"

"Amazing?"

"Yeah. There's something…"

"I know. At first, I thought it was just me. The mother thing. But he seems to cast a spell over everyone he looks at." Shauna bit her lip.

Kristy frowned. "Are you trying to say it's not a cuddly baby thing, but that he's actually doing something to us?"

Shauna glanced away and back. "Of course not. I'm just not used to how people love babies."

Why didn't Kristy believe that?

***

Kristy grinned with satisfaction at the two remaining pancakes and one sausage left on the serving plates. She thought she'd made too much, but Jason had wolfed down the meal like a starving man.

Jason threw his napkin on his plate and stood. "Thanks, Kristy. That was good."

"You're welcome."

He leaned down in front of Shauna and kissed her. "Bye, honey." He kissed Logan's forehead, and ran his finger down his cheek. "See you later, little buddy."

After the front door closed, Kristy jumped up and took Logan from Shauna's arms. After holding the warm bundle a few times, she'd become more comfortable with Logan. "Go relax on the couch, and I'll put this little guy in the bassinet."

Kristy followed Shauna's slow steps to the living room and stopped beside the basinet at the end of the couch. "His front or back?"

"Back."

Kristy lowered the baby into the bed and watched him

for a few moments. His eyes squished tight and his lips pursed. She was sure he would cry, but his features relaxed. "I'm going to clean up the kitchen."

"Thanks for coming to help me, Kristy."

"Hey, what are best friends for? Look how much you helped me when I broke my arm in that gym accident in seventh grade."

Shauna squinted. "Are you comparing a baby to a broken arm?"

"No! Just, we help each other when needed."

"You saved that one."

Kristy sauntered to the kitchen to clean up and loaded the dishwasher, then returned to the living room with her tablet and a notebook. Shauna had curled up on two cushions and fallen asleep. Kristy settled at the end of the couch and turned on the tablet.

She logged onto her favorite puzzle site. The cryptogram she'd done the week before had been quite the challenge. All the words of five or more letters had been written backwards as well as in code. It had taken quite a while to notice that the words made sense in reverse, but overall, when completed, the paragraph had made no logical sense.

She started the new cryptogram, but it didn't take long to realize it required the same key to solve as the week before. She screeched. "This is ridiculous." Without thinking where she was, she tossed her notebook onto the coffee table. Just as it would have landed, it paused and flew into Shauna's hands.

Kristy sucked in a breath. "What just happened?"

Shauna scooted up against the corner of the couch. "That's what I was going to ask. You woke me. You don't know how tired I've been from waking in the night with Logan. I might have sent you packing if you'd woken Logan."

Kristy's gaze darted to the bassinet. Not a peep. Good. "How did my notebook fly back to you? It's not like it's a ball. Besides, it didn't hit the table."

Shauna handed the book to Kristy. "Um. I can levitate."

"What? Are you serious?" She glanced where the notebook should have struck, then back to Shauna. Maybe Shauna was still asleep and dreaming, and Kristy had dropped into it. Like that made any more sense. "Of course you are. And you never told me this—why?"

Shauna bit her lip. "Okay. So, after I arrived in Rawlins, I got special abilities. One of them is levitation."

"One of them? What else can you do?" Was she really talking about magic powers to her best friend? They were immersed in a superheroes movie. "We've been best friends since kindergarten. When were you going to tell me?"

"Never. Sorry. It's just too weird, and I didn't want it getting out."

"Hey, you know I can keep a secret. How many times did we do something we weren't supposed to, and I never told?"

Shauna laughed and pointed a finger. "You were always the one to talk me into doing it, and you would have been in trouble, too, if you told."

"Yeah, well. I still didn't tell. What else can you do?" They hadn't seen each other much in the last year, but they talked at least twice a week, and in all that time there'd been these new powers Shauna had.

Shauna drew in a breath and let it out slowly. "I can also create protective bubbles."

"What does that mean?" She'd never expected her friend was more different from her than she already knew.

"Imagine a soap bubble around something, but this one can prevent bullets, fire, or just about anything from getting inside it."

This wasn't the normal kind of secret like back when they had crushes on boys at school, but still, Shauna should have trusted her with this secret. "Prove it."

Shauna narrowed her eyes. "Okay." She sat up straighter and held out Kristy's notebook. "Throw this at me."

Kristy hefted the book. It wouldn't hurt if it hit Shauna. And of course, it would hit her. She tossed it at her friend's chest. Shauna didn't lift her hands to catch it, but it hit an invisible wall and slid to the couch.

Kristy leaned forward and ran her hand along a smooth but squishy surface, like a pool cover over water. "Wow. I can't see anything."

Her hand slipped through and landed on Shauna's arm. "It's gone now?"

"Yes."

Kristy propped a fist on her hip. "If I stay in Rawlins long enough, will I get magical powers, too?"

"We call them abilities. No. Not unless you have relatives who lived in Salem."

"All my relatives are from the south."

Shauna shrugged. "So, probably not."

"Does that mean that Jason has...abilities, too? And his family?"

"Yes. Kathleen has the strongest and most abilities of anyone for centuries. It was pretty intimidating at first, but I really like her."

"And I bet she adores you. Especially since you've given her a grandson. I can't imagine having a mother-in-law who could turn me into a toad."

Shauna slapped Kristy's thigh. "She wouldn't do that."

This conversation was getting weirder by the minute. "You said wouldn't and not couldn't. Does that mean she could if she wanted to?"

Shauna squinted. "I don't think so. I've read through

some of Kathleen's spell books, and I've never seen one that can turn a person into something else. This isn't a fairytale."

Kristy leaned closer and lowered her voice. "What can Jason do?"

Shauna glanced to the side, as if Jason was skulking behind the furniture. "He can see in the dark."

Kristy chuckled. "I can do that pretty well."

"No. I mean, as if he's wearing those night vision goggles."

"Hmm. That's useful for a PI. What else?"

"The other thing he can do is make lightning."

Kristy pointed toward the window. "Like he can point at a tree and say 'hit it'?"

"It's a little more involved than that, but yeah. Now, tell me why you threw your notebook?"

"Last week I worked on this challenging cryptogram. It was amazing. But it turns out that the one for this week uses the same key. How ridiculous is that? I thought I'd have a couple of hours of fun, and instead it's plug and no play. And they don't even make sense."

"That's frustrating. Let me see it." As kids, they used to work puzzles together. Shauna had never been as good as her.

Kristy flipped her pages. "Hold on. Let me finish solving this one." It took a few minutes to fill in all the proper letters under the mixed up ones on her paper and transfer the solution to the screen. She hit enter on her tablet, then turned to the previous page and handed her notebook to Shauna. "This is last week's solution."

Shauna's eyes widened as she read through the words. She flipped the page and her gaze traveled down the sheet. "This is a description of a spell. And not a nice one."

Kristy covered her mouth. "People not only have abilities to float things and make bubbles, they can mix together spells like love potions?"

"Yeah. Sort of. Kathleen would know more about it than me, but she and Reese are on vacation."

With this new insight, Kristy read through the two weeks of ciphers. "This is kind of convoluted, but it sounds like someone could put a spell on a room full of people and induce them do whatever the spell-caster told them to."

"That's what I got from it, too."

Kristy sucked in a breath. "And I just sent in this week's solution." She tore the sheets off her notebook and wadded them up. "I'm not solving any more puzzles on that website. There's no way I'd contribute to whatever evil someone could be planning."

"At least this was only the description. The instructions and ingredients weren't included."

Logan cried and Kristy waved between Shauna and the bassinet. "Can't you float him to you?"

Shauna's eyes widened. "I'm afraid I'd drop him."

Kristy lifted him from his bed and held him out to Shauna.

"Can you change him first?" She pointed to a diaper station set up on a table beside the couch.

Kristy held the baby to her chest. "Me? This is the first time I've touched a baby and you expect me to change him?"

Shauna grinned. "A week-and-a-half ago is the first time I changed a baby, and I feel like an expert now. You'll do fine. Just make sure you keep him covered so you don't get peed on."

"What?" She'd watched Shauna change Logan's diaper a few times, and it didn't seem as hard as she expected.

All while she changed him, though, her thoughts remained with the cryptogram spell. She hoped no one else would solve the rest of it.

Chapter 2

Kristy paced Shauna's living room. She'd sent the last cipher solution ten days ago. She wished she hadn't sent it without thinking. Two days ago, her morning email had included a message from the puzzle website reminding her there was a cryptogram to solve. They'd never done that before. She'd gone on vacations or been too busy to work out solutions and never gotten a peep from them.

She received their request, reinforcing the notion something nefarious was going on. Never again would she go to that website. She had two other puzzle sites that would slake her thirst for a challenge.

She stopped at the far side of the room next to a familiar bookcase and ran her hand over its side. A pleasant smoky cherry scent tickled her nose. She plucked out a book and sniffed the spine. Yes. Shauna's father had owned these books. He'd never smoked his pipe in their presence, but his home office always smelled of cherries tobacco. It was nice that Shauna had kept some of the furnishings and mementos from her childhood home when it was sold.

She shoved the book back into its slot. Shauna's father should have had a chance to enjoy his grandson—if his life hadn't been cut short by Shauna's ex-fiancé.

"Hey, do you want to go to lunch today?"

Kristy spun around to find Shauna dressed in something

other than sweats for the first time since she arrived two and a half weeks ago. Logan wore the cutest little outfit. "You sure you're up to it?"

Shauna lifted one shoulder. "I hope so. I'm going stir crazy. Soon you'll be gone, and I'll have to do this anyway."

Kristy nibbled her lip. "Um. Maybe not."

Shauna's brows popped up. "Why not?"

"I...got fired just before I came. I figured I'd job search here in Rawlins. After you were well enough."

"How many jobs have you—"

Kristy pointed a finger. "Don't even go there. Too many."

Her two week vacation had become a permanent separation from her employer. Too many irritations had become an argument with her boss on the day before she was to leave. It was fine. She'd been there three years. Longer than any other job she'd held.

Shauna grinned, and side-hugged her. "I'd love for you to live nearby. You know you can stay here as long as it takes to find a job and apartment."

"I've missed having you down the block like when we were kids."

"Me, too. Come on. Let's go." She retrieved an infant carseat from the front closet and knelt beside it. She lowered the baby into it, but the belts were too tight. "I guess he's grown a lot since we brought him home." A quick adjustment made it fit just right. Shauna stood with her hand on the handle.

"Here, let me carry it." Kristy picked up the precious cargo and followed Shauna out the door.

"Jason already installed the carseat base." She opened the back door. "Just set it in and wiggle until it clicks."

That done, Shauna dropped a diaper bag and her purse on the floor, then they got into the car, "It feels good to get out. Now, where shall we eat? I'd love to go to Reese's place, but I don't want to drive that far yet."

"It's out of town, isn't it?"

"Yes. In town, we've got the *Black Kettle Restaurant* and *Cozy Corner Diner*."

"Let's go to the *Black Kettle*." Diner food didn't appeal to her, at least not at the moment.

In less than ten minutes they parked at the restaurant and were seated in a corner with Logan's carseat in the booth beside Shauna.

"Ignore them," Shauna said.

Kristy frowned. "Ignore who?"

"Whoever's staring at us."

Kristy tipped her head as if she was reading the menu and lifted her eyes to scan the room. A good share of the other diners watched them. Shauna's back was to the room, so it would be easy for her to ignore everybody, but Kristy faced them. She leaned over the table. "Why are they staring?"

"Because it's a small town and you're new. I got the same treatment my first six months. Even after they all found out my grandmother grew up here and I'm descended from the founders."

"Jeez. It sounds like you're royalty."

Shauna giggled. "It's not like I'm the queen of England. There were seven families." She waved her hand over her shoulder. "Probably half the people here are descendants."

Kristy shook her head. "Let's forget about them and eat."

The waitress returned, and Kristy ordered a soup and sandwich combo.

Shauna handed over her menu. "I'll have a turkey sandwich. It'll be easier to handle if Logan wakes up."

Kristy shook her head. "This baby stuff is a lot of work."

Shauna was enchanted by her son's sleeping face. "But

it's worth it." She grinned. "And I love watching Jason with the baby."

That was sweet—watching the big, stern man holding the tiny infant in his arms with as much love on his face as for his wife.

That's what Kristy needed. It had taken her long enough to figure out. All the short-term relationships that fizzled because she couldn't commit, too scared to open her heart. And the many hook-ups where she craved a warm body, not understanding what she really needed.

She propped her chin on her hand. After the last breakup, the only one that really counted, it had taken weeks for her heart to break and for her to realize what she'd done. She'd had a rule—no more than two months with a guy, then they were through. That wasn't long enough for anyone to touch her heart. But Kristy had been wrong.

She'd even gone to a psychologist, not understanding her depression. That had been the best money her dad had ever spent on her. Kristy's mother had loved her but couldn't have realized how screwed up she'd made her daughter with all her affairs. Kristy adored her father but never told him about her mother's indiscretions because she couldn't be the one to devastate him.

She rubbed the back of her head and cleared her thoughts.

Shauna raised her brows. "What?"

"Nothing." That was one secret she'd never shared with her friend. "Here comes our food."

Throughout the meal, they chatted about general things, and the baby didn't cry until Shauna's last bite. She whisked him to the restroom to change him, and once she returned, they shared a dessert while he nursed.

Kristy carried the sleeping baby in his seat back to the car and snapped it into place. They buckled in and headed

13

home.

Shauna yawned. "I can't believe how tiring that was. It was good to get out, but I need a nap."

Kristy chuckled. "For once I'm the one with more energy. I'll do laundry and start dinner while you two sleep."

"Wonderful."

Shauna pulled into the driveway, and Kristy got out. She opened the back door of the car and leaned over Logan's carseat to unhook it. She lifted it just as a burly arm wrapped around her neck and forced her backward. Hot breath fanned her ear, and her body locked up, but her hand held firmly to the baby seat.

"Put the kid down or I'll crush his skull."

The arm tightened on Kristy's throat, allowing barely a wisp of air into her lungs. She nodded, and he loosened his grip as she lowered Logan to the ground. She'd choke before she let this man harm her godson. At first it seemed like a weird carjacking, but the assailant wasn't on the driver's side.

Across the roof of the car, Shauna's face blanched. "No! This isn't happening again."

She flicked her wrist and the man jerked forward and grunted. His arm released her and Kristy shoved him as hard as she could. She snatched up the carseat and ran toward the house.

Shauna waved her hand again and Kristy glanced over her shoulder. A rock hurled itself from the pile surrounding the mailbox post, striking the man's head. He dropped to the ground.

Shauna spread her fingers. "There. That should hold him." She leaned against the car and took her phone from her purse. "Jason, we have a little problem. Someone tried to kidnap Kristy."

Kristy's heart gave two loud thumps. The man had been after her?

Kristy heard Jason's frantic voice, but couldn't make out what he said.

"No, we're fine. I put him in a bubble, so he can't do anything more."

Kristy studied the man but didn't see the bubble. She wasn't about to poke it like before. It still seemed like he could get up if he was conscious, but he wouldn't be able to grab her. Two softball sized stones sat on the ground near him. That woman had a pretty accurate throw or levitation or whatever it was. Shauna had saved her. Kristy sank to the ground.

"All right. I'll call the police and break the bubble as soon as they get here. Bye, honey."

The baby woke while Shauna talked to the police. Kristy untangled him from his seat straps and hugged him, patting his back. She paced between Shauna and the house. She didn't know why someone tried to take her. She hoped it was random. Whatever the reason, Logan could have been injured or kidnapped with her.

As soon as Shauna finished her call, she held her arms out, and Kristy handed Logan over. Shauna soothed the baby and paced in front of her car while Kristy kept her gaze on the man on the ground. She wasn't as sure as Shauna that the bubble would hold.

The police arrived and took their statements, then dragged the man away. Apparently, Shauna had popped the bubble, because the cops had no problem picking up the guy. They'd been impressed that Shauna had hit him with a rock.

As the police car drove off, Jason's car flew into the driveway. He jumped out and ran to his wife and hugged her with the baby sandwiched between. "Are you all right?"

Kristy was the one who'd nearly been taken, and he hadn't even looked at her yet.

Shauna leaned back and held up four fingers, going into

a rant. "Four times. That witch bitch must have jinxed our house."

Kristy didn't know what Shauna was talking about, but already Kristy didn't like whoever it was, and she wondered if the woman really was a witch.

Jason took the baby from Shauna, held him in one arm and rubbed Shauna's arm. "Honey—"

She pointed to her feet. "It all happened here. First, I was kidnapped, then Jamie was kidnapped." She held up two fingers. "Twice! And now someone tried to kidnap Kristy."

Kristy hadn't heard about Jason's sister being kidnapped a second time. That must have been terrifying after being missing a month the first time.

Shauna's voice quavered. "When your parents get home, I want—"

Jason wrapped his arm around his wife. He tugged her tight against his side and kissed her forehead.

Neighbors who had come outside to check out the police incident drifted back into their houses. Yeah, they didn't need to witness Shauna going crazy. She'd been strong the whole time until Jason embraced her.

Shauna dropped her head to Jason's shoulder, her voice filled with anguish. "I almost lost Kristy."

He rubbed her back. "But you didn't. You saved her."

"I didn't save Jamie and Trill."

Who the heck was Trill?

"Nobody blames you, and it worked out in the end."

Shauna tipped her head back, her eyes wide. "Maybe it wasn't Vanessa. Maybe it's me. Or she cursed me. I was with all of them when it happened."

Jason turned her around and started walking toward the house. "All right. We'll see what Mom can do when they get back."

It sounded like humoring Shauna to Kristy, but it calmed

her down.

It used to be, the women knew, or knew of, everybody the other was acquainted with. Now, parts were a mystery. They hadn't shared everything in their phone calls.

Kristy scanned the yard and street, still unsure why this happened. No one had a reason to come after her. It must have been a random attempt. And if that was the case, it was done.

She locked and closed the car door, picked up the baby seat, then followed the others into the house. Jason and Shauna climbed the stairs, and Kristy headed to the laundry room. After starting the washer and dryer, she was startled by Jason standing in the doorway, his mouth in a firm line.

"In my office. Now!" He stalked away.

She had a sense of foreboding, like one of the two times she'd been sent to the principal's office. Only this was worse.

Kristy forced each step that drew her closer to Jason's office. She shouldn't feel guilty for what happened. Someone attacked her. But Jason's anger loaded her with guilt.

She stopped in the doorway.

Jason sat behind his desk with his arms crossed, glaring at her. "Sit."

Shauna's desk chair had been moved in front of his desk. She dropped into the chair, surprised by how low it was. She'd used Shauna's chair before, but now the height must be at its lowest. She wasn't playing this game. She glared back and raised the seat to a comfortable height.

He dropped his palms to the desk and leaned forward. "You put my wife and son at risk today. What are you involved in?"

"Nothing! I don't do drugs. I don't sell drugs." She threw her hands up. "The only thing remotely illegal I do is occasionally speed."

"Then why did someone try to kidnap you?"

"Well it certainly wasn't for the same reason Jamie was kidnapped. Or Shauna." She pointed a finger at him. "Which happened on your watch." If he was going to accuse her of something, she'd throw it right back at him.

For a moment his façade cracked.

"I'm sorry. I shouldn't have said that."

He blew out a breath. "I blame myself, too. So, you don't have an ex who might do this?"

"Seriously? The only real ex I have is…wouldn't do this." She wouldn't go there.

He quirked an eyebrow.

"And I don't have hoodoo magic, so no one's coming after me for that."

He smirked. "We just call them abilities." At least, he seemed to have calmed down.

"Well, the only"—she used air quotes—"ability I have is solving puzzles. It's not like that's going to get me into trouble."

He leaned back and stared at her. She returned it with a glare.

Then it clicked, and the warmth drained out of her body. She actually checked the floor to see if she'd sprung a leak.

He leaned forward. "What? You just thought of something, didn't you?"

She nodded. "I belong to some online puzzle clubs."

"And?"

"My favorite is cryptograms. One site had the hardest puzzle I've ever done. I was so excited to try out their next one, but it was the same key. How stupid is it that they didn't create a new one? I showed the solutions to Shauna, and she said it was the beginning of a magic spell. A really dangerous one. I wasn't going to solve any more of them. After a few days, I got this email reminding me that a puzzle was waiting for me. Those sites don't do that. They don't care who solves them."

He crossed his arms. "If they're the ones, you solve their puzzle and they won't come for you again."

"Seriously? Two weeks ago, I didn't even know this witchy stuff existed, but now, there's no way I'd help someone use that spell."

"What does it do?"

She stood. "I'll get my solution." She ran from the room and raced up the stairs, and into her room. From the top of the dresser, she collected crinkled pages she'd decided not to throw away and, at the last second grabbed her tablet, then headed back downstairs. She hadn't solved any puzzles since the day she'd found out about the spell.

Kristy dropped the sheets in front of Jason. "Here."

She sat, crossed her legs and bounced her foot as Jason scrutinized the pages.

He glanced up. "Yeah. You don't want to finish this puzzle." He stared at her hands. "Can you show me the emails?"

Kristy opened up her email program and searched the website name so only those messages would show up. She held the tablet out to him.

He took it and touched the screen. A frown marred his face. Jason lifted the tablet. "Do you mind if I keep this until morning? I might be able to track where these originated."

"Sure. But wait." She snatched the tablet back and opened a browser and typed in a web address. "Here's the website with the creepy puzzle." She handed it back.

He glanced down, then up at her. "Thanks. I'm sorry I was so…"

She stood. "I understand. You have to protect your family. I should pack and go home."

He vaulted to his feet. "You can't. They'd find you for sure." He ran a hand through his hair. "Let me come up with something that will keep you and my family safe."

"Okay. Thanks for being understanding." She escaped to the kitchen to start dinner. Probably the last one she'd make for the Ballard household.

She would never intentionally have done anything to hurt Shauna or Logan. She would rather have gotten kidnapped than have them injured.

***

Mark Simmons opened his duffle bag over the washer and tipped it on end. His toiletries bag caught his eye, and he grabbed it before it could follow his clothing into the washer. He'd been gone for nearly three weeks to some godforsaken jungle and absently scratched an itch on his neck. Yeah, he could do without mosquitoes the size of small birds for a while. He closed the top on the washer and trudged up to his room, dropped the bag in his closet, then fell face first onto his bed.

Lately, there'd been too many missions, but it was his own fault. For the last seventeen months, he'd asked for a new assignment as soon as his boots hit U.S. soil. This time, his boss told him no, he needed downtime.

Too much time on his hands gave him a chance to think, and when he wasn't on a mission, his thoughts turned to Kristy. Nope. Not going there. Maybe after he woke up, he'd go to a bar and find some company.

His eyes couldn't have been closed more than a few minutes, when the vibration and chime of his phone woke him. He should have turned it off. It was already dark out. He fished the offending object from his pocket, surprised at his caller.

He sat up. "Hey, Jason. How's that little family of yours?"

"Great. And I want to keep it that way. I want to hire you."

"Timing couldn't be better. I just got back from a mission today." And now he'd have a way to keep busy so he wouldn't think about…that woman. "I can't believe you need help keeping your wife safe. I thought you had employees now."

"I've got two employees and another is coming on board next week. But this isn't something I can trust any of them with. They don't have the kind of expertise you have. I need the best, because Shauna would kill me if anything happened to her best friend."

Mark's insides felt like they'd been dumped on the outside. "Kristy? Nope. Sorry, buddy. You're going to have to figure out something else."

"Look. I know you two dated for a couple of months, and she can be snarky sometimes, but can't you put up with her for a couple of weeks?"

Snarky? Only in a cute way. Mostly sweet and kind and funny. Perfect. Until the day she told him they'd hit their time limit, and she walked away, the morning after giving him the best night of his life. It came out of the blue, and he'd been gutted.

"No."

Jason sighed. "Someone tried to kidnap Kristy from my driveway today. With my wife and son there. The guy even threatened to hurt Logan if Kristy didn't go with him."

His heart stuttered. He shouldn't care. "So, what happened?"

"Shauna hit him with a rock. And, um, put him in a bubble to contain him until the police arrived."

Mark massaged his temples with his thumb and ring finger. "Bubble? Is she in the habit of giving bubble baths in your driveway?"

Jason chuckled. "It's an ability—like I have. The bubble protects like Kevlar but is flexible like Mylar."

Mark shook his head. "How did you find a woman with powers like you?"

"Hey, you're the one who set me up with Shauna."

"To protect her. I'm not a dating service." He wished Jack Collins hadn't asked him to find a bodyguard for his daughter's best friend. He never would have met Kristy and been screwed over by her.

"Anyway," Jason said, "Kristy's gotten mixed up in solving a cryptogram. She solved two parts before she realized it was a…magic spell. A really bad one."

Mark flopped back on the bed. "Spells? Like when Reese became invisible?"

"Yeah. Only this one, the wielder could make a roomful of people do whatever he wants. Can you imagine what that would do in the hands of the wrong person? Or anybody, for that matter."

Mark rubbed his chest over his heart. "She can hide out for a while. They'll find someone else to solve it for them." Thoughts of when Shauna's ex went after Kristy passed through his mind. Mark had taken Kristy to a Caribbean beach resort. He shoved the memories away, not wanting to remember how fantastic it had been between them.

"Do you really want that kind of power in some bad guy's hands?"

"Oh, so you're being altruistic, too? Isn't there some kind of Justice League for taking down bad guys with powers?"

Jason laughed. "Not that I know of. I called on you when we found Jamie and had to rescue her from that lunatic."

That guy had been plain creepy. Mark wouldn't want Kristy to go through what Jamie had. And if this group got their hands on her, it would be worse. Once she solved their puzzle, they wouldn't need her anymore. They'd be more likely to kill her than release her. A world without Kristy would be a dimmer place.

"All right. I'll do it." He hoped he wouldn't regret it.

"I appreciate this, man. Since Mom and Dad are away, I'm putting you two into their house. I don't want my family exposed to any more danger."

"Will they be okay with that?"

"They'll be fine. I'll have Tony stay with us or Jamie. Abby can stay at school instead of coming home on weekends." Good idea to get Jason's brother and sister out of harms way.

"Okay. Let me catch up on sleep tonight and I'll be there sometime tomorrow."

"That works for me. Thanks again, man."

Mark dropped his phone beside him and put his arm over his eyes. Kristy. He couldn't believe he'd be seeing her again. He wished he had some kind of power to put a shield around his heart.

Chapter 3

Kristy vaulted from the table and dropped her fists on her hips, glaring at Jason. At least they'd gotten through her wonderful dinner before he dumped it on her. "Absolutely not! Call him back. Tell him not to come. I'll go hide somewhere."

Jason crossed his arms over his chest. "First, if they found you here, they'll find you anywhere. Second," his gaze slanted to his wife then back to Kristy, "Shauna would never forgive me if something happened to you, and I didn't protect you. And third, Mark already agreed to do it. I don't know what happened between you two—" He held his palm up to her, "and I don't want to know, but he doesn't want anything to happen to you either."

She flattened her hands on the table. He seemed so composed, and she felt out of control. It was hard to believe Mark would want anything to do with her.

Shauna stared at her, concern in her eyes. "I want to know."

She couldn't have all that come up right now. Sometimes they teased each other like sisters, and other times they stood together against adversity. They were the most unlikely of friends. They would never have become friends if they'd met in high school, but they were fast friends by that time.

Kristy's gaze returned to Jason. "I'm going to take care

of the dishes." She stacked plates and grabbed two glasses. "Then I'll pack."

Shauna began to get up. "I'll help."

Kristy rested her hand on Shauna's shoulder. "No. You rest." Even after her rest, exhaustion shadowed her eyes. Having to dispatch the bad guy on her first outing had drained her.

It didn't take long to fill the dishwasher and put away leftovers, then Kristy headed to her room. She had planned on doing some online job searches in Rawlins the next day, but she'd have to put it off. Kind of hard to go on job interviews when she was in hiding.

She set her suitcase on her bed and opened a drawer. The door behind her closed and Kristy spun around. "I'm not surprised to see you. Where's the baby?"

Shauna plopped down on the bed. "He's getting daddy time. Here, let me help." She waved her hand and a pile of clothes left the open drawer and landed neatly in the suitcase.

Kristy sat beside Shauna. "How much energy does that take?"

"About half as much as actually doing it."

"I've got clothes in the closet, too."

The closet door swung open and clothes slipped off hangers and folded themselves, floating one by one to the suitcase.

"That is so cool."

Shauna kept waving her arms. "What happened with Mark?"

"First, you tell me about Vanessa, the witch." Maybe a distraction would make Shauna forget.

Shauna bit her lip and glanced at the closed door. "You can't tell anybody."

Kristy grinned. "Girl, you know I can keep secrets."

"We ran into Vanessa where she worked at *Cozy Corner*.

From that moment, she tried to get Jason back."

"You mean, they dated?"

Shauna nodded. "For a couple of months in high school. He dumped her. She used spells, and even had some kid switch his medallion for one she'd put a spell on. My ex had tracked me to Rawlins, and when he showed my picture to Vanessa, she told him I was living with Jason."

"Oh, my god. I can't imagine how angry he was."

Shauna wound her hands together. "Yeah. It was bad. Anyway, after Jason rescued me from him, Vanessa confronted us in the front yard. She ranted about how her mother told her Jason was supposed to be hers. I didn't know what kinds of abilities she had, and when she started to wind up like she was going to use one on either Jason or me, I put her in a bubble."

Kristy grabbed one of Shauna's twisting hands. "What happened after that?"

Shauna squeezed Kristy's hand. "Lightning shot out of her fingers and ricocheted around the bubble. By the time it ended, all that was left inside was a pile of ash at the bottom."

Kristy hugged her friend. "You didn't do that."

"I know. I tried to blame myself, but Jason convinced me that we might have been killed, and I acted defensively. She did it to herself."

"Who else knows?"

"The old man across the street saw it, came out and said, 'Good riddance.'"

"So, now Vanessa is a missing person?"

"Yes. Forever." Shauna sucked in a deep breath and ran her hands down her thighs. "End of subject change. What happened with Mark? I figured he was like any other guy you were with for a few days or weeks before going onto the next. Because you never told me anything about it."

Kristy sighed. "I was afraid you wouldn't forget." She flopped back on the bed. "I broke up with him, but not soon enough. I hurt him." She rubbed her eyes. She wouldn't cry. She'd done enough of that in her therapist's office.

Shauna rubbed Kristy's arm. "Why'd you breakup with him if you love him?"

Kristy tucked her lips. There wasn't much she hadn't told Shauna, except for what happened with Mark, and that great big secret she'd take to her grave. "Because it would hurt him more later when I cheated on him."

Shauna's eyes widened. "What? You've never cheated on a guy. Why do you think you'd cheat on him?"

"That's because I never stayed with anyone long enough to get bored with him or whatever causes someone to cheat. I figured if I stayed with Mark long enough, I was bound to."

Shauna took her hand. "Honey, that doesn't even make sense. Why do you think you'd do something you've never done before?"

"Because…because…I just do." Nope. Not telling her mother's secret.

"So, how many *dates* have you been on since you dumped Mark?"

Yeah, Shauna knew her history. Kristy couldn't count the number of times she'd had hookups from the clubs and bars she frequented. Some of those had become boyfriends for a few weeks. And guys she worked with and others at the coffee shop. Sexy, interested guys were everywhere. Before talking with the therapist, she didn't know why she needed that or even that it was a need.

"None."

"Aha!"

Kristy jumped. "What?"

Shauna slapped Kristy's leg. "Don't you get it? Starting in high school, I don't think a week passed that you didn't have sex at least once. And it's been how long?"

She studied her hands. Maybe it was time to redo her nail polish. "A year and a half."

"See! If you"—she stabbed a finger at her—"can go that long without sex, then you'd do fine having sex with just Mark. You wouldn't cheat."

"But—"

"No buts. Kristy, this is your chance to try again with him. Explain to him whatever it is that is scaring you." She glared at her friend. "Whatever it is that you won't tell me. Maybe you two can work through this."

Kristy sat up and wrapped her arms around her legs. "You just want everybody blissfully happy the way you are with Jason."

Shauna grinned. "I want you happy. And you were for a short time with Mark."

"I burned that bridge."

"Build a new one. Maybe you only have to go halfway."

"Yeah, I can see that. I build halfway and then plunge to the rocks below." Mark wouldn't trust her after she'd hurt him. In spite of Shauna's encouragement, she still didn't trust herself not to hurt Mark again.

***

Mark rang Jason's doorbell. He still couldn't believe he'd agreed to guard Kristy. The best way to deal with her was to make sure they were rarely in the same room. They'd have ground rules. The Ballard home was very secure, so he didn't need to be on top of her all the time. He groaned and rubbed his temples. Bad choice of words.

The door opened and Jason stretched out his hand. "Thanks for coming, bro."

Mark shook his hand, and they clapped each other on the

back.

Jason stepped back. "Come on in. You're just in time for supper."

"Great. I'm starved." He hadn't had much real food in the jungle.

Maybe a small dose of Kristy while everyone was around would be a sort of vaccination against her when they left together. He could only hope.

The tingle as he crossed the threshold didn't surprise him anymore. He'd experienced it the first time at Jason's parents' house. Jason had been surprised he'd felt it when he asked what it was. Magic spells protected both houses. Not that it had done much good with the number of kidnappings the family had experienced.

He followed Jason into the kitchen, and froze, his breath stuck in his lungs. Kristy set a platter on the table and met his gaze. It didn't seem possible, but she was more beautiful than he remembered. And not so…vibrant. Maybe she still hadn't recovered from almost getting kidnapped. Her wavy blonde hair was longer than he remembered, and he liked it. Those blue eyes could be icy, merry or sultry. Mostly sultry, and he needed to forget that.

"Hi, Kristy."

"Mark." She fled into the kitchen.

Maybe if she couldn't stand to be in the same room with him, it would work out. Jason's parents owned a big house. If he made sure to eat at different times than her, they could go days without seeing each other. It wasn't the normal way he conducted a guard detail, but he didn't normally have to protect himself, too.

A female sigh behind him had him spinning around. Shauna held the baby on her shoulder with a cloth under his head. "Hey, Mark. Thanks for coming."

"Hey, yourself." He took a step closer and touched the

baby's cheek. Miracle baby. He glanced at Jason's contented expression. The man who was never going to have kids. "You did good for yourself."

Jason wrapped an arm around Shauna's waist. "I did."

Kristy's voice drew their attention. "Dinner's ready." She had finished putting food on the table with a choice of beverages. He remembered like it was yesterday, the delicious meals she'd prepared for him. And pot roast was his favorite. Had she made it for him? He couldn't go there.

He stood back as Shauna tucked the baby into a bassinet on wheels against the wall, and everyone sat. Jason took the head of the table with Shauna on his left and Kristy beside her. Mark took the empty place to Jason's right. At least he didn't sit directly across from Kristy.

Jason speared a slice of beef. "I talked to Dad this morning, and everything's all set at their place. They'll be gone two more weeks."

Mark grabbed two muffins. He didn't know what Kristy did to make them special, but it was another thing he missed. "We should have it resolved by then." Hopefully, just a couple of days, and he could get out of there.

"You still have access to safe houses, just in case?"

"Uh, yeah." He'd make sure they wouldn't be together that long. "Once we get settled, I'll start tracking back from the emails and website. It shouldn't take long to locate these guys."

Shauna scooped mashed potatoes on her plate, then poured gravy over them. "Can we talk about something other than those creepy guys? Even football would be better."

Jason smirked, and Mark was pretty sure that Shauna didn't like football. Kristy, on the other hand, had cheered alongside him. The time he'd surprised her with tickets to her favorite team's game, she'd been ecstatic.

He'd done so well blocking her out the last few months,

and now he'd have to start over again. "Shauna, the yard looks nice. Is that your doing?"

She nodded, grinning. "Thanks. The yard had nice bushes when we bought it, but I added the flowers. I used to tend the flower beds in the house where I grew up."

Kristy snorted. "And she used to rope me into helping her."

Shauna poked her with an elbow. "You never complained."

"Of course not. I wore a bikini top and short shorts and got whistles from passersby."

Jason coughed like he'd choke on something. Mark wished he could get up and walk away. She'd probably done him a favor by leaving. All Kristy seemed to want was good times and nothing serious.

Shauna kept the conversation rolling through dinner and brownie sundaes for dessert.

Mark stood. "Thanks for dinner. Kristy, we should get going."

Kristy pushed her chair back. "Let me get my bags."

She returned, wheeling a medium sized bag, a smaller one over her shoulder, and a purse over the other.

Mark pointed at the two women. "Okay, you two. No phone calls on Kristy's cell phone. You have free rein on the Ballard's house phone." He and Jason had tried before to keep the two off the phone and that had led to near disaster with Shauna's life.

Shauna squeezed his arm. "Thanks for leaving us a line of communication."

"You're welcome."

The women hugged. He still found it hard to believe these two were such good friends.

At the same time, they said, "Love ya." Then stepped back.

Outside, Mark stored Kristy bags in his car. "Follow me over, but you won't be driving once we get there."

"Fine."

Five minutes later, he pulled into the half-circle driveway in front of the Ballard house. Mansion, as far as he was concerned.

Kristy stopped behind his vehicle as he got out. He grabbed both their bags from his backseat and marched to the front door, Kristy following behind. Hot shivers ran up his spine as he strode into the foyer. The Ballards must have refreshed the protection spell before leaving. Since the bad guys wanted a spell decrypted, they had the capability of performing other spells, and while in the house, Kristy would be protected from those.

Mark locked the door and continued across the open space. He jogged up the stairs and stopped beside the first open door. Kristy reached the top, and he pointed at the room beside him on the left and then the next one. "Choose a bedroom. This one or that one." He was fairly sure she would choose the more feminine room.

She grabbed her rolling bag, then grasped the bag from his shoulder. His bag slipped off and dropped on his foot. "Ouch!" Yes. Always hurting him.

Her gaze dropped to the floor. "Sorry. I didn't do that on purpose."

"You sure?"

Her head snapped up. "Of course, I'm sure. I'll take Jamie's room."

"Make sure the windows are locked."

She entered the second room and closed the door.

He'd let her think she'd had a choice. If he'd told her which room would be hers, she'd have insisted on taking the other. His intention all along had been for him to take Jason's room, the first one at the top of the stairs. No one would get past that door.

He dropped his bag on the bed, and extracted his laptop, then tapped twice on Kristy's door. "I need your laptop and that puzzle solution."

Kristy opened the door and held out crumpled pages in one hand and a tablet in the other. "I already opened it to email and loaded their website on the browser."

He took the items. "Thanks. Now give me your passwords in case I have to access it when you're not available." Like when she was sleeping. She appeared beautifully innocent in sleep.

She propped her hands on her hips. "As if I'm going shopping or something. Just ask when you need it."

"Just give it to me." He glared at her, and she turned her head away.

She sighed and closed her eyes. "It works for both. PiratesCove4MS. Caps on P, C, M and S. Numeral 4." She slammed the door in his face.

Rooted to the spot. Stunned. MS were his initials. He'd had two glorious weeks with Kristy at *Pirates' Cove*. Perfect weather, perfect beaches, perfect…nights. Why did she still have that password?

He swore. She made no sense.

Mark searched all the bedrooms, making sure the windows were locked, then ran through the dormitory style rooms on the third floor, checking windows.

Back on the first floor, he headed to the library. A fireplace was set a few feet to the left of the double-doors. Beyond that, bookshelves ran to the corner and along the far wall and across from him, ending opposite the fireplace. Two places were interrupted with windows, one a window seat. Who the heck had a library in their home that someone would walk in and say, "This is a library?" No one else he knew. He'd been here a half-dozen times before, but it still amazed him. Jason had never acted like he came from money.

A seating area of plush couch and chairs were arranged at the far side of the room, another in front of the fireplace. Midway between them sat a table with two green shaded library lamps. He'd use the desk. It had a view all the way to the front door. He couldn't see the stairs, but once Kristy stepped off them, he'd see her. He set the tablet and laptop on the desk, then checked all the windows on the first floor. The sliding glass doors in the kitchen had an additional security lock that was engaged.

He sunk into the desk chair in the library, and as his laptop booted up, he read over the puzzle solution and key, impressed Kristy had solved it. He'd never had the patience for puzzles. Give him a mission with the intricacies of planning its success any day, something that was real-world and worthwhile.

After pondering the puzzle, he understood Jason's concern. He couldn't imagine the damage that would be done if someone used the spell on an entire police force, or governing body. What if they strolled into the Senate chambers and cast the spell? The Supreme Court, or any court, for that matter. And whoever this was had pinned everything on Kristy solving it for them.

He rubbed circles into his temples, then swiped the screen on Kristy's tablet. Once GPS tracking was turned off, he felt a bit better. She'd left the last puzzle email she got open. He read through it and checked for others. Only two. Nothing before this particular puzzle. If he didn't know by the near kidnapping, this told him it was definitely important to someone.

He had a twinge of guilt, but still made a quick search for messages from men, and only found ones from her father. It shouldn't make him feel better, but it did.

On his laptop, he poked around on the website. They had

a list of older puzzles, but the ones Kristy had done weren't there. Back on her tablet, he clicked on the link in one of the emails. It took him to a website that initially appeared exactly as the one on his laptop, but there were subtle differences. The puzzle list included the older ones displayed on his laptop, but the more recent ones were for the spell puzzles. Interesting.

In a browser window on Kristy's tablet, he typed in the website address, the same as on his laptop, but the page it landed on was the same as the one linked in the email. They'd somehow hijacked her tablet.

He deleted the two email messages, then deleted them from the trash. Her virus protection program was outdated, so he downloaded an update for it, then started an install.

Meanwhile, he carefully typed the mock website into his browser bar and entered the site, then opened a special program and set it to search out the origin of the website. It might take a while.

Mark started the anti-virus program to search for viruses and headed up to bed—in the room beside Kristy's. What woman would have a password that reminded her of the guy she broke up with?

Maybe he'd finally get answers. While finding out who wanted to kidnap her.

Chapter 4

Kristy entered the bathroom with her clean clothes over her arm. She wasn't surprised the room was steamy. No matter what time he actually got to sleep, Mark always rose early. And she didn't want to think about how, for a short time, she'd been his reason for staying up late.

She hurried through her shower and dressed, not bothering with makeup since she'd be avoiding Mark, anyway. Not that no makeup stopped him from wanting morning sex when they'd been on that Caribbean island. She'd give anything for them return to the way they'd been.

The coffee aroma drew her to the kitchen. She found mugs behind the second cabinet door. As she reached for the coffee pot, she noticed a note sitting in front of it.

Breakfast in the oven. Please turn it off.

She grinned, remembering the times he'd cooked breakfast for her, and wondering what he'd made this time. She poured coffee and dumped the expired milk down the drain. She'd have to see if Mark would let her go grocery shopping. Oven mitts sat on the counter, which she used to grab a plate of scrambled eggs and a couple sausage links from the oven, setting them on a cloth placemat at the table. She thoroughly enjoyed the meal, never expecting to experience Mark's cooking again.

After cleaning up, she found Mark sitting at the desk in

the library, typing on his laptop. She stood in the doorway, drinking him in. The expressions crossing his face reminiscent of those times he worked while they were together—the squinted eyes, grim mouth, and occasionally rubbing his temples between his thumb and fingers. She had excelled at distracting him from work.

She sighed and stepped into the room. "Morning. Thanks for breakfast."

His gaze tipped up to her and back to the desk. "Good morning." He lifted her tablet. "Here. I cleaned up the viruses. Don't go to any puzzle sites." He fixed his eyes on her. "I'm keeping your phone, so you don't make any calls from it."

She snatched her tablet and hugged it to her chest. "I wouldn't. You already said to use the house phone."

He narrowed his eyes. "Yeah. Like you weren't supposed to call Shauna when her ex was searching for her? Remember how that turned out."

She flinched. It pained her anytime she thought about Shauna's abduction since it had been Kristy's fault Shauna's ex found her. "I learn from my mistakes."

His gaze bore into her. "Yeah, me, too."

Tears pricked her eyes, and she looked away.

"I started a grocery order on your tablet. Finish up what you want and put it through. I already added my credit card info. If you finish by ten, we'll get the delivery this afternoon." He resumed typing on his laptop again.

Dismissed, she stalked to the window seat halfway across the room and dropped into it, practically invisible. He hated her. She couldn't blame him. They'd been really happy together. She'd almost decided to break her two month rule and risk a longer relationship. Then her mother happened, reminding her of all the reasons it was a bad idea.

Kristy wiped her eyes and dragged in a long breath. It

was too late for them, and she had to deal with it. A tap on her tablet screen, and entering her password, reminded her of the surprise on Mark's face when she gave it to him. Hopefully, he just thought she didn't want to remember a new password.

Once the grocery order was placed, Kristy tried to read, but her mind kept wandering. She wanted to work a cryptogram, but the fun ones were on the websites she frequented. She had to settle for a cryptogram app on her tablet. They weren't nearly as complex a challenge but would keep her occupied for a while, and maybe keep her mind off Mark.

***

Mark had gotten nothing accomplished in the last couple hours, not since Kristy entered the library. It shouldn't bother him that he'd hurt her by referring to her as a mistake. She'd tried to hide the misting of tears, but he'd seen them. Maybe the real mistake had been to let her go without a fight. Their ending had been too abrupt. Looking back, he realized something must have prompted the breakup, but at the time, he'd been too heartbroken to focus deeper.

His stomach growled, and he checked the time. Nearly noon. Groceries wouldn't arrive before lunch, so he searched for a local pizza shop and found one that took online orders. Sausage, mushrooms, and jalapeños, Kristy's favorite.

Forty minutes later, the doorbell rang. Mark stood as Kristy eyed him. He pointed at her. "Stay over there."

He collected the pizza and a two-liter soda, and carried them to the kitchen, not having decided if he'd eat at the table with Kristy or take his slices back to the desk.

This was worse than his most awkward bodyguard assignment. In that case, he'd been guarding a princess who tried every way she could to get into his bed. He wasn't interested in spoiled brats, especially one whose fiancé had hired him. Fortunately, the situation was resolved in three days, and he'd hightailed it out of there, wishing the fiancé the best of luck.

Most of his dates were with women he'd run into while socializing. One night or a couple of weeks with them, it was cool. Sometimes, a while later, they met up again, but it was no big deal either way. Kristy was different. He couldn't do a repeat with her. Maybe that first night with her had been about sex, but he hadn't walked away. Mark wasn't even sure if he regretted it.

He set the food on the table and got out dishes. A noise had him glancing to the doorway where Kristy hovered.

"Come eat." And he still hadn't decided if he was eating with her. He flipped open the box.

"You remembered my favorite."

Like he could have forgotten anything he'd learned about her. He put ice in the glasses from the refrigerator door and poured soda. Kristy dropped a slice of pizza on her plate and sat. He grabbed two, and hesitated. She raised her brows.

Several times, they'd sat together sharing pizza or some other meal, sometimes starved after making love. They'd laughed and talked and touched.

He picked up his plate and glass. "I can't do this." He stalked back to the library.

Moments later, Kristy raced across the open foyer, bolted up the stairs, and slammed her door shut.

He let out a long breath. It seemed all he could do was hurt her now. He picked up his phone and selected Jason's number.

"Hey, did you find anything out?" Jason's voice was way too cheerful.

Mark rubbed his temples. "I can't do this. You need to

find someone else."

Jason barked out a laugh. "It hasn't even been twenty-four hours. You're it, man. There's no one else."

Mark dropped his head against the back of the chair and closed his eyes. He didn't need this type of gut-twisting assignment. His best bet was to get it done as quickly as possible. "I tracked the emails to the puzzle company. It's someone who works there, or someone who hacked into their servers."

"That's a good first step."

It wasn't, unless the emailer really worked there. "I'm researching the company, and I'll run background checks on the officers."

"Great job. I have some bad news."

The whole assignment was bad news. "What is it?"

"The guy who tried to kidnap Kristy is dead. Found hanging in his jail cell."

"They think it was suicide?"

"It's inconclusive. But either way, someone doesn't want anything about this spell getting out."

All of this over some magic spell that he shouldn't even believe was real. And Kristy was in the middle of it with proof now that someone had, willingly or not, died for it.

***

Kristy had imagined it would be hard seeing Mark again, but even after eighteen months, this was so much worse. He hated her. Couldn't stand being in the same room with her.

If she'd known how empty and heartsick she'd feel after breaking it off with him, she might have let it run its natural course. Then he could have gotten on with his life without being so angry with her. Nothing could have made it worse for her.

She had to figure out how to fix this. If only emotions were as easy to figure out as puzzles, she'd have a happy life.

Still, it wasn't that bad. She had happy parts. Her best friend had a bad couple of years after her father died, but now Shauna was over-the-moon in love and with a family. And little Logan was the most adorable baby ever. That made Kristy happy.

Her dad made her happy. He always had. They'd done so many fun things together when she was growing up, and he was the one who'd gotten her started solving puzzles. He'd had a rough time after her mother died a little over a year ago, but he'd found a new woman, and she was so good for him. Kristy really liked Jessica. Her dad had been so nervous when he introduced them, it had made her giggle.

So, there was happy in her life, but the biggest part of it right now was full of pain. She'd thought a few dinners would help, but Mark did everything he could to avoid her.

She lay on the bed, staring at the ceiling. Her tablet was in the library, so she didn't have anything to do. Maybe Abby had some books in her room and wouldn't mind if Kristy borrowed one. She peeked out the door, and not seeing Mark, crept into Abby's room. She felt a bit guilty entering the private space, but she wasn't going to borrow clothes—just a book.

A stack of paperbacks sat beside the bed, and Kristy squatted beside them. Most of them were sci-fi. She could work with that. She lifted the stack, minus one, and scooted the bottom one over before setting the stack down again. If Abby was working her way through, she wouldn't miss this one for a while.

Back in her room, Kristy, propped up on pillows, started reading. It was a sci-fi romance. A short time later, voices drifted up the stairs, and Kristy cracked the door open to listen. The groceries had been delivered. If they were on speaking terms, she would have helped Mark put the food away, but she'd let him do it himself. He could cook, too. She'd sneak down later and have that pizza she missed out on. If he didn't want to spend time with her, she'd do her best to accommodate.

Kristy waited until Mark retired for the night before going downstairs. He had left her a plate of food in the refrigerator. While she waited for it to warm in the microwave, she wandered the kitchen. The door to the half bath off the kitchen was open. Usually it was left ajar. Now, seeing to the back wall, it seemed too close. She stepped into the doorway to the library and studied the distance to its back wall. They should both be the outside wall.

She counted out the steps from the kitchen doorway to the back wall of the bathroom, then counted the same number of steps from the library doorway. She finished about eight feet from the wall. She cocked her head and inspected the area. Not surprising that an old house like this had a secret room.

With no obvious entry from here, she hurried back to the bathroom. She pushed, prodded, and ran her fingertips over the wall in search of crevices. Nothing. Then on the side walls, she sought out buttons, switches, and slides. Anything that might open a hidden door. Still nothing.

Not deterred, she ran back to the library. No secret room would defeat her. Starting in the corner, she ran her hands over the wallpaper, one at hip level and one at shoulder height, feeling for indentations. Her upper hand hit it first, a seam. She ran her fingers up the crack. It took a turn at near normal door height and dove down the other side. She'd found it!

Now, to get in. She ran the palm of each hand on either side of the seam from one end to the other. Nothing. She stepped back and examined the wall. Maybe the closest picture hid the lock. She tried to nudge it, but it seemed fixed to the wall. Instead, she ran a hand under the frame across the bottom. Nothing. About halfway up the side, there was a slight indent. She peeked under but couldn't see it in the dim light. A gentle poke with a fingertip caused a click and a door popped open a half-inch.

Kristy grinned. She'd done it. Her fingers fit snuggly into a crevice on the edge of the door, and she pulled it open on silent hinges. She found a light switch to the right of the door. A bare bulb illuminated the eight by eight room. A half-filled bookcase sat across from her with a small table and two chairs in front of it. To the left, a recliner and floor lamp filled a corner.

This was an ideal hideout. In times past, when the house didn't have indoor plumbing, there'd probably been a chamber pot or something similar in here for long-term hiding. Now, no one would want to hide for more than a few hours. She approached the bookcase. Most of the books were about witches and spells. There were a few journals. Some seemed really old. Maybe the real reason for the secret room was to hide the books. It would be fun to peruse them, but she should ask Shauna first.

She closed up the room, and grabbed her tablet from the window seat. She removed her warm dinner from the microwave, then headed up to her room. The late night meal would probably keep her awake even longer. And by the time she was ready to fall asleep, she'd have spent too much time thinking about Mark, which would lead to lust filled dreams about him. Again.

Chapter 5

Mark rubbed his temples. He'd gotten exactly what he wanted when he accepted this assignment—he and Kristy ignoring each other—and now that it had played out, he didn't want it. He absolutely hated it and was miserable. Kristy had taken the painful hint he'd doled out and run with it, literally. Over the last five days, he'd barely seen her, and when they did end up in the same room, she turned tail and ran.

The first evening, he'd made dinner and hoped to apologize, but she never showed. As he stored the leftovers, he'd checked the pizza box and discovered she'd taken some. She must have eaten it cold since he hadn't heard the microwave. That night, Kristy must have snuck down to retrieve her tablet from the window seat in the library.

The following afternoon, Kristy puttered in the kitchen, and he thought he might get a chance to clear the air with her. She noticed him, and before he had a chance to stop her, she raced out of the room, and her footsteps pounded up the stairs.

That evening, her voice, flat and not warm like it used to be, drew his attention from the online search he'd been conducting.

"Dinner's ready."

His heart leaped. Maybe they'd get a chance to talk. His

gaze found her, and his heart plunged. She carried a plate and glass, and turned away, heading for the stairs. She'd made his second favorite, meatloaf and scalloped potatoes. She'd probably had wonderful plans when she put in the grocery order, but he'd ruined it all. Every bite was an indictment of his cruelty, and he couldn't enjoy it.

Each day since had been similar. This was worse than the days after she broke up with him. In the same house, but farther apart than ever.

The doorbell rang. First time since the grocery delivery, and he hadn't ordered anything. He stopped at the kitchen doorway. "Kristy, hide just in case."

She scurried into the library, sliding the pocket doors closed behind her. The room didn't have a good place to hide, not even a closet, but the person at the door was probably harmless.

Mark peeked out the window beside the door. A man, about his height, in a suit with a briefcase in his hand, stood on the porch. Maybe this was someone Reese knew who didn't realize he was away. He couldn't turn away Reese's business associate or client without a face to face explanation.

Mark opened the door. "May I help you?"

"Yes. I'm here to see Kristy Collins. I have a substantial offer for her."

Mark stiffened, hands splayed at his sides. It would only take a moment to pull the gun from his back waistband. He hadn't expected a direct approach.

"There's nobody by that name here." No way would he let this man near her.

One corner of the man's mouth tipped up. "I know Miss Collins is here, and I'm sure she'll be interested in our offer."

Mark didn't know how they'd found her, but the man wouldn't get a chance to make his offer. "I'm sure she won't be."

"I've got cash incentive. I'm sure that will make all the difference."

"Not with Kristy." Mark started to close the door.

The man's face contorted with anger. "That's not how this is going to work." He swung his briefcase forward in an arc and chucked Mark in the chin with the bottom corner, causing him to step back to catch his balance. It must have been full of bricks. Before Mark could recover, two men in jeans and black t-shirts swarmed in.

The suited man dropped his briefcase. "Take care of him while I find the woman." He marched toward the library.

"No!" The blond man grabbed Mark's right arm, but he punched just as well with the left, and before the dark haired man could grab him, Mark hit the guy in the jaw, sending him stumbling back onto the porch. Mark slammed and locked the door. Dealing with Blondie alone would be easier. He grabbed the gun from his waistband, a bit of a fumble since it was tucked in for right-handed use. He aimed it at Blondie's heart and the man released him. "Take your shirt off."

The man's eyebrows rose. "Ooh, sex on the first date."

"In your dreams. Get the shirt off."

Blondie yanked it over his head and Mark snatched it from him, then spun the man around and slammed him face first into the front door.

Mark tucked the gun into his waistband, slipped the man's hands through the neck and into the sleeves of the shirt. A tight fit, but all the better. He wrapped each side of the bottom around the wrists, and tied them tight together. It would do until the police arrived. He had zip-ties in his car, but never thought he'd need them in the house. He yanked the man around, so he faced the room. "Call your friend out here."

Blondie glared and yelled out. "We got a situation out here."

Mark noticed Blondie didn't use a name. No one responded. He hooked Blondie's ankles with a foot and shoved him forward. The man dropped with a grunt onto his chest. Mark hoped he broke a rib. Then he whacked the back of the man's head with the butt of his gun. That should keep him out a while.

He dialed 911 and informed the operator he needed the police. After he hung up, he screamed Kristy's name as he raced for the library. One of the doors was already open. He shouldered the other back and rushed into the room, and took a slow spin, searching for places she might have hidden. "Kristy!"

If the suit had captured her, she would have put up enough of a ruckus that Mark would have noticed the guy dragging her out. Unless she'd been knocked out first. But he still should have noticed.

He ran to the kitchen. His heart sank at the sight of the outside door wide open. "No!" He sprinted through the door, and the gate in the privacy fence. Two heads were visible in the car racing for the corner, both bulky males. Kristy might be unconscious on the back seat or in the trunk. The license plate was too far away to read.

He hurried back into the house, hoping to find her somewhere. He called out and searched the rooms on the first floor. The fact that she didn't come out of hiding had him more worried by the minute that they'd taken her.

The doorbell rang and he hurried to answer. Two policemen stood on the porch. Mark kicked Blondie's foot. "This guy's buddies may have kidnapped my girlfriend."

The officers stared down at Blondie. The one on the left chuckled. "Pretty creative tying there."

"Yeah. I learned it in MacGyver class."

The officers chuckled.

Mark didn't have time for this. "You know Jason Ballard?"

The second officer waved a hand around. "Who doesn't know the Ballards?"

"Call him. He's got the details on what's going on. I'm checking the rest of the house in case my girl's still hiding."

The officer shook the guy's arm. "We'll take this guy in and come back to take a statement and make sure you found the girl."

Mark waved them off. "Fine." He sprinted up the stairs, stepped into every room and checked closets and bathrooms. Nothing. Each room he checked, his fear mounted. If she'd been hiding up here, she would have responded by now. He'd almost had her back. At least, they'd been in the same house, and he'd still had a chance. Now, she might be gone forever. He might not survive losing her like this.

Third floor. Jason had said that long ago it was servants' quarters. He raced up the stairs. Every room gave him a second of hope, but Kristy was nowhere.

He dialed Jason. "I think they got her. I told her to hide, but I can't find her anywhere."

"The police called. I told them enough but not too much. Later, you're going to have to go in and give a statement. Did you check the secret room?"

Mark halted halfway down the stairs to the first floor. "What secret room?"

"Shauna didn't tell Kristy about it, but this is Kristy. She may have figured it out."

The oppressive weight in his chest eased a bit. "What. Secret. Room?"

"It's accessed in the library."

Exactly where Kristy had run, and he'd dismissed it as the worst place to find sanctuary.

The police and the suspect were gone from the foyer. He ran into the library, scanning the room. "Where?"

"Back, right corner."

"I don't see anything." This had to be it. The perfect hiding place. If anyone could find it, Kristy would.

"Last picture on the right. Left side, under the frame, there's a depression."

Mark ran his fingers up the wall under the frame, and they delved into a small dip. He pushed it and where there'd been no door, one popped open a half-inch. He pried it the rest of the way open. His gaze lit on Kristy, sleeping in a recliner with a book on her lap.

He choked up, and his voice was gruff when he spoke. "Found her. Thanks." He ended the call. He'd have to let the police know she wasn't missing, but that would have to wait until after he held her.

As he stepped through the doorway, the hot zing of a protection spell zipped up his spine, ten times worse than the one at the front door. He sucked in a breath. Man, he didn't want to do that very often. It was worse than the time he'd accidentally touched an electrified fence. Peace and calm hit him, then the quiet. No wonder Kristy hadn't heard him calling and had gone to sleep. She probably hadn't been sleeping any better than he had and needed it.

He squatted beside the chair and ran a finger down her cheek. He hadn't touched Kristy in eighteen months. The small touch added to the peace that filled him from the spell.

"Kristy. Baby, it's safe now."

Her eyes popped open, and she studied him, a wrinkle between her brows. She must have seen something different in his face than he'd shown her lately. She launched herself at him, and he tumbled backwards. Kristy in his arms was something he'd never expected to feel again. He kissed her, drinking her in. It'd be a long time before he had his fill. Her body pressed into his, and every hot fantasy flashed into his mind that he'd had since seeing her again. Something niggled, telling him they needed to talk. This room would help her release her secrets, keep her calm enough to reveal her worries. And that was more important to their future happiness than fulfilling their lust.

Mark struggled to his feet, not wanting to let Kristy go. He dropped into the recliner with her snuggled on his lap. He tipped his cheek against her head. "I love you, baby. I'm not letting you go this time no matter how hard you fight it."

"Mark, I time limited you, so I wouldn't cheat on you."

Judgment and anger wouldn't get the answers he needed, and somehow, this room helped him control it. Now was the time to get all the details and figure Kristy out. "So, you found another guy and left me so you could have sex with him?"

Her head rubbed his chest. "There wasn't anyone else. I just knew it would happen eventually."

"How many guys have you cheated on?"

She stiffened. Maybe he'd already gone too far.

"None. But you're only the second guy to get time limited. Nobody else was around long enough, or they were just hookups."

That's what he and Kristy should have been. A quick, convenient hookup. It had become so much more.

He didn't need to know, and didn't really want to, but the question shot out of him. "How many guys have you been with since you broke up with me?"

Silence. He'd definitely overstepped with that question. He hadn't been celibate. At first, he'd had revenge sex, as if she'd know or care he'd been with someone else. It had evolved to normal sex, but it wasn't normal, at least not the way it was before Kristy. It hadn't felt right since her. Guilt didn't make sex fun. He'd given up on it months ago.

"None."

His arms involuntarily tightened around her. None. She'd been more loyal than him, and she'd been the one to break up. "Baby, if you can go eighteen months without sex, you can manage making love with only me. Why do you think you'd cheat?"

Silence again. He was beginning to think he wouldn't get this answer, and he thought it was an important key to Kristy.

She lifted her head and stared into his eyes. "You have to promise not to tell anyone." She paused. "No one at all."

He held up two fingers. "Scouts honor." He pinched his thumb and forefinger together and ran them across his lips. "Lips are sealed. No one at all."

She dropped her head back to his shoulder. "I haven't even told Shauna. The only one I've told is my therapist."

He'd have to ask her about the therapist later, because he didn't need it to sidetrack him now.

"I'm afraid I'm like my mom."

"Your mom cheated on your dad?" In all the years he'd been friends with and worked with Jack, he'd never had an inkling the man had a troubled marriage. Maybe a little. The only time he'd met Riana, the woman had run her gaze over him as if she wanted to eat him. He'd turned his back to her.

Mark cupped her cheek and kissed her briefly. "I met her. You are nothing like her. She was a cold bitch, and I don't know how your dad couldn't see that."

"He loved her, and she was a totally different person with him. I think, in her own way she loved him, too. Just not enough to wait around while he was on missions."

"Are you sure?" He had no trouble believing it but wished she didn't know that about her mother. It may have been what had messed up her perception of relationships.

"Yes. From the time I met Shauna, Mom used to instigate sleepovers for me at Shauna's house when Dad was away. That's one of the reasons Shauna and I became such good friends. One evening when I was twelve, Shauna and I had a fight. I don't even remember what about, so I ran home."

He held her tighter. It was long past, but he wanted to let her know he cared.

"I heard voices, and I thought Dad was back. Their bedroom door was open. I stopped in the doorway. They were naked with their backs to me. But it wasn't Dad. Mom's back was to this guy's front, and he was kissing her neck and talking to her."

"Aw, honey." Mark kissed the top of her head. He couldn't imagine what he would have felt if he'd witnessed a similar scene with one of his parents. This was why she'd rarely talked about her mother but bubbled over with stories about her father.

"I left as quietly as I could and headed back to Shauna's. After that, I knew that anytime she had me stay at Shauna's, she was with another guy."

"I'm sorry, baby. Is this related to your time limits?"

She nodded. "I didn't want to cheat." Right there told him she wasn't like her mother, but she didn't see it.

"Our last night, I got to the restaurant early. I heard Mom laughing in the bar. She was wrapped around another man and didn't notice me. I left and waited on the bench for you."

"That's why you wanted to go someplace else."

"I didn't want you to find out about Mom, especially since you know my dad." She dragged in an uneven breath. "It reminded me I was like her, and I should leave you before I hurt you."

He kissed her forehead. "It was already too late."

"I'm sorry. I didn't expect it to hurt me, too, but I deserved it."

"What you deserved was to have a better mother." He

wondered if it was intentional to act like her mother with all her lovers.

He'd had his fair share of hookups, and a number of short relationships, but on the whole, he'd been searching for the right woman. He just hadn't found her until Kristy, and that had ended in heartbreak.

He lifted her chin and waited until her gaze met his before speaking. "Let's put to rest that fear of cheating. You haven't done it. You're not going to. Let's see where we go from here."

She bit her lip. Her eyes mesmerized him. Finally gave a nod.

He was sure there was more Kristy hadn't told him, but she was exhausted from telling this secret that had shaped her life. He'd leave the rest until after they were comfortable together again.

He shoved the lever to lower the footrest and stood, letting Kristy get her footing before releasing her. "Come on. Let's make dinner. Afterwards, I'll give Jason a call, and we'll come up with a plan to stop these guys."

He hit the light switch, and they stepped together through the doorway. That horrible tingle coursed through him. He hoped he wouldn't have to experience it again.

"What was that?"

He closed the door, making sure it latched securely. "What was what?"

"That tingle."

"You felt it? It's the protection spell around the secret room."

She squinted. "I didn't feel it going in."

"I sure did. You felt it through me."

She grinned. "Really? Maybe you've got some witchy blood in you like the Ballards."

Chapter 6

Kristy snagged the cordless phone from the library desk while Mark took care of the dishes after a cozy breakfast. She raced upstairs to her room and dialed Shauna's number, laying back on the bed, staring at the smooth ceiling. She couldn't count the number of times the two of them had talked this way.

Back in high school, although Shauna knew Kristy was sexually active to the extreme, Kristy only talked about the boys she'd dated more than once. She hoped Shauna didn't know that Kristy had done a good share of the football and basketball teams every year from the time she was sixteen.

Through the therapist, she had a better understanding of herself, and wished she could go back and repeat high school and college. Maybe she'd have been happier if she'd been more like Shauna.

Nah. Maybe somewhere in between.

The call dropped into voicemail, and she waited through the message, and gave her own. "Hey. I'm going to try again."

Next time, Shauna picked up on the third ring. "Hello?"

"It's Kristy."

"I figured it was you."

An ear-piercing wail made Kristy yank the phone from her ear, and Shauna said, "Hold on a sec. I'm diaper changing." The crying continued for almost a minute, then stopped abruptly. Must be feeding him.

A long breath swooshed out of Shauna. "Soo, have you gotten Mark in the sack yet?"

Kristy chuckled. "I can't believe you're asking that. But I guess that's what married life does to you. And the answer is no."

"Oh. You don't sound upset like the last time we talked. Are things going better?"

Kristy grinned. "Yeah. Did Jason tell you how Mark thought I'd been kidnapped?"

"No! What?"

"I'm not surprised your husband wouldn't want you to get upset. After those guys left, Mark couldn't find me, and he said he was pretty frantic by the time Jason suggested the secret room."

"I didn't tell you about that room."

Kristy chuckled at indignant Shauna. Sometimes it had taken some coercing to get Shauna to do some things, and other times, nothing worked. Probably those times when it was a really bad idea.

"I found it myself. Anyway, it was so peaceful in there, and I hadn't been sleeping well, so I fell asleep. Mark found me, and he looked…like I was his present."

"Aw. So you're back together?"

Kristy huffed out a breath. "Sort of. We're talking again. And he doesn't seem to hate me. I think we're kind of like friends." She'd never had guy friends before. "But we slept in separate rooms last night."

"Oh. Um. You know it was a long time before Jason and I, um…"

Kristy laughed. "Yeah, Virgin Queen, I know. And it probably only happened because you dreamed about sex with him. I bet that had to do with your witchy stuff, too." She waited, but Shauna didn't respond. "Anyway, Mark and I did it the night we met. We barely knew each other's names, so there's no comparison. I'm just afraid he doesn't want me that way anymore. Maybe he's friend zoned me."

"Give it time. If he's talking, you've got a chance to get through to him."

And maybe worm her way into his heart. Turnabout was fair play.

"Tell me about my godson. Is he sitting up yet?"

Shauna laughed. "You make it sound like you've been gone for months and not a couple of weeks. He's not even two months old. But he's smiling."

"And I'm missing that?" She'd never thought much about babies. She didn't have siblings. Shauna didn't either, so she hadn't spent much time with younger kids. Being around little Logan had given her a longing she never expected.

The lifestyle she'd had didn't allow for attachments, except for Shauna. But once she moved away, there was no one to consistently count on. Being with a guy for a night or a couple weeks didn't chase away the loneliness. That had been obliterated by Mark. And it had scared her. After he left— after she kicked him out of her life, the loneliness had been worse than before. She now knew what it was like to have a man who cared about her and she cared for.

She'd ruined it and might never get it back.

"Hey, how about if I ask Jason if we can come over for dinner?"

Kristy sat up. "That would be great. Just let me know the day before so I can get groceries delivered."

"Okay. Love ya."

"Love ya back."

Kristy flopped back on the bed. Her clothing choices were limited to pretty much house cleaning clothes—jeans and leggings, t-shirts and a couple of tanks. If she'd known Mark would show up, she could have packed sexy clothes to lure him back.

***

Kristy slid the pan of lasagna into the oven then prepped the vegetables for the salad. Two days since she and Shauna had tentatively planned the dinner. From what Shauna said, she'd had to do some wheedling to get Jason to agree. Kristy giggled, wondering if Shauna had withheld sex to get what she wanted, but couldn't imagine it. She didn't know how long after having a baby you could have sex again, but Jason probably felt like he hadn't caught up yet.

"Hi, you two." Shauna's voice filled the foyer.

Kristy raced out of the kitchen and caught her friend in a hug. She stepped back and stopped Jason to lean over Logan's carseat and kissed the baby's forehead. "I can't believe how much I've missed this little guy."

Jason sidestepped her and set the carrier next to the wall in the kitchen.

"Hey, Jason." Mark and Jason shook hands.

Shauna nudged her arm and whispered. "Here."

Kristy stared at a plastic grocery bag her friend handed her. "What's that?"

Shauna leaned in. "Sexy clothes. You can thank me later by telling me if they work."

She whispered back. "You don't own sexy clothes."

She made a snatch for the bag. "Hey. I can take these back."

It wasn't a good idea to offend someone bearing gifts. "Well, not my kind of sexy clothes."

"That's why I bought these for you online." She grinned. "You should have seen how disappointed Jason was that they weren't for me." Her gaze dropped to her waist. "I still have to lose more weight to fit into most of my clothes." She slanted a glance at Jason. "But I've got some great ideas for new clothes."

Kristy hugged Shauna. "Thank you. I'll run them upstairs."

She emptied the bag on the bed. They were similar to the club clothes she had in her closet. A couple of weeks after breaking up with Mark, she'd tried going to a club and a couple of bars. Those three nights, she felt out of place, like a different person. She'd danced with some guys, but the excitement was gone. Some had asked her to leave with them. Her body used to tingle from anticipation before leaving with her chosen, but disgust filled her and she'd refused them all. Her bed had been a lonely place ever since, but there was only one body she wanted warming it.

By the time Kristy returned, Mark had poured wine into two glasses. Jason already held a beer and another sat on the counter. She stopped in the kitchen doorway. Her heart squeezed at the scene. It was as if she and Mark were a couple having another couple over for the evening. Playing house. It wasn't real, and she didn't know if it ever would be.

Shauna spotted her. "Is there anything I can do?"

"Why don't you and Jason figure out where you want to eat and set the table?"

Kristy washed her hands and glanced over her shoulder. "Sorry I don't have homemade rolls." She lifted a package of brown-n-serve rolls.

Mark grinned. "I love those. I'd take them any time."

He probably said it to make her feel good, and she loved him more for that.

Shauna and Jason talked quietly as they collected place settings and left the kitchen. Mark leaned against the counter beside her and took a drink from his bottle. "Thanks for putting this together. I think we all needed it."

"Thank you for agreeing. I really needed my Shauna fix." She glanced at the sleeping baby. "And that little guy over there."

As if he'd understood her, Logan woke and cried. Mark hurried to the seat and expertly removed the baby, lifting him to his shoulder. He patted the small back, and Logan quieted.

"Wow. You're good at that." She expected Mark would be afraid to touch a baby that small, but he acted like an expert. She never thought that a baby in his arms would thrust his sexy score to eleven.

"I have twin nieces. They're four. When I visit my sister, no way am I allowed to get out of helping. Besides, I figure my godson should get to know me."

The tray of rolls slipped from her fingers and clattered onto the counter. "I'm going to kill Shauna." Since before Logan was born, Shauna had plotted to put her in an awkward situation with Mark.

Mark chuckled. "You jumped from needing a Shauna fix to wanting to kill her in the space of ten seconds. What gives?"

She studied his face. "He's my godson, too."

One of his eyebrows twitched. "Well, let's hope that they both live a really long time."

She frowned. How was she supposed to take that? They couldn't get along well enough to take care of a child together? Would they have to shuffle Logan back and forth like divorced parents?

Before she could respond, he was beside her. "Hey, I didn't mean that the way you're taking it." He kissed her, way too briefly. "I wouldn't mind if we had to raise Logan together. I just meant I don't want anything to happen to Jason and Shauna."

She blew out a long breath. "Okay." She slipped away

from him and shoved the rolls into the oven, setting the timer. Shauna was going to get a talking to about not telling her that Mark was also a godparent.

Jason and Shauna returned to the kitchen, her cheeks flushed. No wonder it took so long to set the table. "Thanks for getting Logan, Mark."

She whisked the baby and diaper bag away.

Jason picked up his beer bottle, took a drink, and rolled it between his hands. "I ran into a friend on the police force, and he was telling me how they were shorthanded because two of their own were in the hospital."

Kristy wondered if Jason wanted to talk about this now because Shauna was out of the room.

Mark frowned. "Are they sick?"

Jason pressed his lips together then blew out a breath. "Those two men were the ones who arrested the dude you took down. They were jacked on the way back to the station and the guy escaped."

Mark's bottle nearly tipped over when he set it down. "And we're only hearing about it now?"

"My man in the station kept putting me off, telling me the guy wasn't talking. And they didn't even have him." He slapped his hand on the counter. "I've used this cop countless times and he's never steered me wrong. I think they paid him off."

Mark shook his head. "Maybe people were listening or he *was* busy."

Jason rubbed the back of his neck. "Yeah, but now I can't trust him. I won't know if he says he's got nothing if it's true."

Kristy gripped Mark's hand. It seemed like he was getting nowhere trying to figure out who these people were. She hated this waiting game. "Maybe I should solve the puzzle for them."

"No!" His and Jason's voices chorused their opinion.

"I don't mean for real. I'd have to really solve it so I know the format and ingredients, and then make something up that is close enough to fool them."

"Baby, that won't work. They'll try it out on a small group, and when it doesn't work, they'll come looking for you, even angrier than before."

"Oh, I hadn't thought of that."

Jason straightened. "Maybe that'll work."

Mark glared and fisted his hands. "No, it won't. I'm not setting Kristy up to be bait any more than she is already."

Jason grinned, and held up his hand. "No. Listen. Shauna and I can write up a similar spell so that when they use it, they broadcast their location to us. It'd be especially good if they try it out at their headquarters."

Mark took a step closer to Jason. "And then what? What if it doesn't work?"

"Would it really be any different than how it is right now? I'm sure every day that passes, they're getting angrier. Whatever plans they have are delayed. We can find out who they are and dig up some dirt on them."

Kristy stepped between them. "I think we should do it."

Shauna returned, a blanket draped over her shoulder. Logan wiggled underneath. "Do what?"

Kristy glanced at her friend. "Send those guys a fake solution to the cryptogram that's actually a locator spell."

Shauna whipped her head around to her husband. "You think we can do this?"

He shrugged. "We can try."

Shauna bit her lip and squinted. "It's not like the spell is in a foreign language. We'd make it deceptive enough to not give away that they're calling us in. And it has to sound like they're turning a bunch of people into robots, but not actually do it. The length has to be the same as the original, or they'll know immediately it's fake." She lowered her eyebrows. "If we do this, we should send it to your mom to tweak."

Mark dropped a hand to Kristy's shoulder. "That's way too much guesswork. And if you sneak in—" he waved his hands in the air "—'hey, find me here', don't you think they'll notice?"

"Not if we word it right, and get Mom to check it over," Jason said.

The oven timer dinged, and everyone pitched in to get the food on the table.

Kristy followed Shauna into the family dining room. She and Mark had eaten only in the kitchen. She wondered if Shauna had been intimidated by the many rooms the first time she stayed in the house with Jason.

Mark arrived last with the rolls in one hand and the baby seat dangling from the other. He set the rolls next to the salad and the seat on the end of the table away from the place settings. That man *did* understand mothers and babies.

Shauna gravitated toward the seat. "Thanks, Mark." She patted Logan's back, and once he burped, she lowered him into the seat. "Kristy, that smells so good."

The couples sat across from each other with the women closest to the baby. The only sound for the next few minutes was silverware clinking as they served themselves.

Partway through the meal, Logan cried.

Mark jumped up and scooped the baby out of the seat before Shauna was halfway standing. "I got this. Enjoy your meal." He patted the boy's back until he quieted, then returned to his seat and took a bite of lasagna.

Kristy didn't think Mark could get anymore sexy, but jumping in to quiet Logan as if it was nothing moved him up a notch. Divorced men with kids had always been a turnoff for her, but maybe it just had to be the right man.

Of course, this was her best friend's baby, but she could

too easily imagine him being a helpful, confident father for their children. That scared her, but not as much as not being given the choice because someone kidnapped her or worse.

Chapter 7

From the library window seat, Kristy stared through the window at the obstacle course set up near the woods, probably from Jason's high school days. Mark's male perfection took her breath away. Muscled legs pumping, wide shoulders bulging, and strong hands that knew everything about how to pleasure her. If he ever got around to doing it again.

Mark jumped over a low bar. Not that low, since she would have gone under it. Next up, he leaped and grabbed a bar with both hands and pulled into a chin-up. She expected he'd drop down to start another, but he continued higher until his hands were straight beside him. He leaned forward and rolled over the bar, and started the routine again.

It was so graceful, he should have been a gymnast. He did five—yeah, she'd counted—before doing twenty regular chin-ups. That's why he was so strong that he'd easily picked her up to have sex against a wall. Way too long ago, but still etched in her memory as if it was yesterday.

He raced off to a slant board where he hooked his toes under a bar and did sit-ups with his hands behind his neck. She could do sit-ups flat on the floor, but there was no way she looked as good doing them. She lost track of counting at thirty-two, imagining sitting on his legs and receiving a kiss each time he sat up.

No wonder he had so much stamina during sex. A hundred or so sit-ups later, he jumped to his feet and raced to a climbing wall. He scrambled to the top and swung over. The angle didn't allow her to see him land, but moments later, he ran to a balance beam about two feet off the ground. He leaped to it, steadied for a moment, then sprinted across it.

In a long expanse of lawn, Mark seemed to stumble, and she gasped. But no, he somersaulted and sprung up, ran ten feet and did it again. And again. The man was crazy.

At the fence, he spun around, dropped to his knees and flat onto his chest. Using his elbows and toes, he belly crawled about twenty feet. She wished she was on the ground in front of him—naked—so he could crawl right on top of her. He jumped to his feet and wove between the obstacles. He made this tough workout seem easy.

She'd only caught it by chance. Shauna and Jason had stayed until ten, then she'd gone directly to bed. Well, after Mark had kissed her and told her she'd been a wonderful hostess and the meal had been delicious. More kisses had left them both breathless, but she hadn't been able to drag him to bed with her. He'd stood his ground, and she'd gone alone and fell asleep immediately. Hence, being up early enough to see his incredible workout. She'd have to try hard not to miss another.

Too bad an elevated heart rate didn't burn a ton of calories. Especially since Mark wasn't giving her the exercise she really wanted. Maybe the new outfit she'd gotten from Shauna would entice him. She'd chosen the darker of the two sets. The top and bottom were snug, a short, black skirt with silver swirls, and a stretchy, black short sleeve shirt that plunged front and back. Not normally what she'd wear at home, but desperate times…

Kristy let out a long breath and dropped her gaze to her tablet. She had a cryptogram to solve so they could find these bad guys and stop them. She scanned through her email messages and found the one from the fake cryptogram website. She clicked on the link, and resumed checking her email.

A message from her father hid among way too much spam. With everything going on and the lack of her cell phone, she'd forgotten about calling him. She clicked on his message.

Hi Kristy,

I haven't been able to reach you and we missed last week's call. Call me ASAP so I know you're okay. I have something I need to talk about.

Dad

Since she had permission to talk to Shauna on the house phone, it should be fine to call her father.

Kristy retrieved the cordless from the desk and returned to the window seat before dialing his number. He picked up on the third ring.

"Hello?"

"Hi, Dad. It's me."

"Kristy! I was starting to worry."

"Sorry, Dad. I'm still in Rawlins." Let him think she was with Shauna. "I broke my phone, and I haven't replaced it yet. I just saw your email."

"How's the baby?"

"He's adorable. And Shauna is so happy with Jason."

"I'm glad. She deserves happiness after what happened to her father." He paused a couple seconds. "So…the reason I wanted to talk to you…"

Kristy sat straighter. "This is more than our regular weekly chat?"

"Well…"

"Dad! Spit it out." It wasn't like him to hem and haw. He was a straightforward type of guy.

"You know Jessica."

"Of course. You've been dating her for, what, six months?" She'd had dinner with her father and Jessica a few times. At first Jessica had been nervous, but Kristy had used every subtle thing she could think of to let Jessica know she was happy they were dating. The woman's bubbly conversation had drawn laughs from her dad and that sold Kristy on her. He deserved happiness.

"Seven months."

"Okay." So precise.

"We're getting married."

Kristy let out a squeal.

"Kris—"

"Dad! I'm so excited for you. I think she's wonderful. And perfect for you. The last time I had dinner with you two, I couldn't stop grinning at the way she looked at you." That was a woman in love. "Congratulations."

"Thanks. I'm pretty happy about it. I wasn't sure how you felt since she's so much younger than me."

Jessica was about halfway between Kristy and her father's ages. "What matters is you love each other."

"I'm happy you're okay with that. Um. There's more."

"More?"

"She's pregnant. With twins."

Kristy squealed again. She couldn't help it. "Dad, this keeps getting better."

"I never expected to have children at forty-eight. You don't mind that I'll have other children?"

"I always wanted to have siblings. This isn't quite the same as I imagined, but I'm going to be a big sister. I love it."

Her dad chuckled. "And to think, I was worried about telling you. All of it. Children aren't always happy when their parent remarries. Or find out about new siblings when they've been an only child for so long."

"Dad, I don't live with you anymore. Even if I did, I'd be happy about it. You'll be an amazing dad, just like you are for me."

"Thanks, honey. We don't have a date for the wedding picked yet, but it won't be too far out."

"Let me know when, and I'll be there."

They talked a while longer before ending the call.

Kristy set the phone down. Her dad finally found someone who loved him, and she was ecstatic. And he'd always wanted more children. She'd once overheard her parents discussing it—how disappointed they were that her mom hadn't gotten pregnant again. Kristy had known for a fact that her mother was on birth control. It would be pretty crazy to allow yourself to get pregnant and not know if your husband was the father.

She jumped up and swirled around, shimmied her hips, and pumped her fists in the air. A chuckle stopped her.

Mark leaned against the doorway, grinning.

She returned the grin and raced across the room. Throwing her arms around his waist, she tugged him away from the frame, spinning around with him. It didn't even matter that he was covered in sweat, and smelling like pure, sexy male. "I am so happy."

He jerked to a stop. "I can see that. What's up?"

She lifted to her toes and kissed him quick. "Dad's getting married."

His eyebrows rose. "Really? Who?"

"Jessica Parsons. She's wonderful for him."

He nodded. "I met her once. She barely took her eyes off him for the introduction." He grinned. "Well, good."

Kristy tried to spin again, but he held fast. "And...they're expecting twins."

"Seriously? That old fox."

"He probably thought he was the reason he and Mom didn't have more kids and wasn't careful, but I think it's great." She hugged Mark tight.

"You *are* happy about this, aren't you?"

"Yes. Mom never loved him enough, and I bet he realizes that now with how much Jessica does."

His arms circled her. "He's a smart man. I bet he's figured it out."

***

After lunch, Kristy and Mark drifted into the library. She sat at the table. Mark slumped at the desk doing whatever he did with his laptop. His computer work didn't seem to bring them any closer to stopping the bad guys. For all she knew, he played video games.

She wrote out the letters and numbers of the third puzzle from the cryptogram site. She started decoding against the key she'd created for the first two parts. After one line, she sat back to read it, and frowned. "Gibberish."

"What?" Mark lifted his brows.

"It's gibberish. This puzzle doesn't use the same key as the other two. That's why they want me. They probably tried to do the same substitution as the first cryptograms and it didn't work." She grinned. "This will be more fun than I expected."

He shook his head. "You should really make a career out of that."

"Seriously? Is there still a call for cryptographers? I thought it was pretty much from World War Two."

He shrugged. "I don't know. But if there is, that's what you should do."

"It'd be a lot more fun than all the other jobs I've done."

"How many jobs?"

69

She lifted and dropped one shoulder. "I lost track. At least ten. Accountant's assistant. Shauna helped me with that one. Receptionist multiple times. Phone sales. I hated it. I do so much better in person."

He grinned. "I agree."

She squinted at him. "Transcriptionist. Dental assistant. Couldn't stand the bad breath. Real Estate agent. Some of the guys got too handsy. Sometimes that was good, other times not so much."

He crossed his arms, and smirked. He knew her past so she wasn't afraid to mention other guys.

"Anyway, I better get this solved." She picked up her pencil and drew a line through the incorrect solution. Back to square one.

She scanned through the lines, trying to pick up on the usual tells. One letter words were the easiest start…but there weren't any. That was unlikely. A check of two letter words found more than the average. Maybe…ah. About half had the same two letters, and she wondered if it was a way to disguise the word 'a'. They might be 'at' or 'an', but puzzles always meant experimenting. She'd have to work the puzzle trying each as the 'a'. There was still the possibility that the words of five or more letters were reversed, or twisted some other way.

She bent to her task, writing the original letters onto a second sheet of paper, and started inserting the letter 'a'. She became immersed in the complexities of the cryptogram, which seemed more convoluted than her life. Progress was slow, but at least she was filling in letters.

Two hands dropped on the table across from her and she jumped, glancing up.

Mark grinned. "Dinner's ready."

Her eyebrows shot up. "Dinner?" It couldn't have been any later than three.

"Yeah. It's almost seven."

"No wonder I have to pee so bad." Although, she hadn't noticed until she'd gotten her mind off the puzzle.

One side of his mouth lifted, but he stayed where he was—half a table away. His brown eyes mesmerized her, and she stood. She leaned across, and it reminded her of the bridge Shauna mentioned they might build toward each other. The two sides were getting closer, but they hadn't met yet. She still might fall off.

All that was forgotten when their lips touched. One of his hands touched her ear on the way to burrowing into her hair. She loved it. Maybe because it was Mark. Or maybe it was the way his fingers kneaded her scalp. She moaned and deepened the kiss.

Minutes later, or maybe it was seconds or hours—she wasn't good with time today—he leaned back. "Dinner's going to get cold. Go do your thing in the bathroom and meet me in the kitchen."

Her cheeks flooded with heat. "Not the brightest idea to mention that."

He chuckled and sauntered away.

Their time together was different from last time. Then, it had been all about the sex. Lots of it. Except her heart had been stealthily giving itself away, piece by small piece. This time the draw was stronger even without sex. And her heart was tearing off larger hunks and smirking at her as it tossed them to Mark. Soon, nothing would be left of her heart to hold onto.

~~~

During one of the times Mark had been distracted by watching Kristy, he decided they should have a movie night. The time they'd been together before, they'd never seen one together, so he had no idea what she liked. While she'd diligently worked, he snuck into the family room and lined up a bunch of movies he hoped she would enjoy.

With a nice dinner over and dishes taken care of, Mark grabbed Kristy's hand. "Let's watch a movie."

She tipped her head. "I should get back to the cryptogram."

"You've worked on it all day. You'll have a fresher mind if you start again in the morning." Maybe it would have worked better if he'd told her before dinner they were calling this a date.

"Okay." She followed him to the family room.

He sat in the corner of the couch and hauled her down beside him. The remote was on the arm where he'd left it. He flicked the huge TV on. "I picked out a bunch of movies. Why don't you choose one?"

Kristy took the remote from him. She cruised through the selection, stopping longer at some than others. At the last one, she backed up a few. "This one."

"Really? You like James Bond?"

She pushed the button to select and start the movie. "I love Daniel Craig. Shauna won't watch these kinds of movies with me."

He took the remote from her and set it beside him. "Spy movies?"

"Spy, mystery, intrigue. I give the plot away. For a while, as soon as I'd start to speak, she'd cover my mouth. Eventually, she refused to watch any of them with me." She shrugged. "So we watch other types of movies."

The movie hadn't started yet, and he was enjoying himself. "You figure out the mystery, huh?"

"Yes. Sometimes I get it wrong, but those times, they messed up."

He chuckled. "It's their fault you didn't get it right?"

She shoved her shoulder into him. "No, it's their fault because they screwed up."

The beginning credits had ended. "Okay. Let's see how this one goes." He'd seen it before, but now anticipated her perspective. He wrapped an arm around her shoulder and pulled her closer.

Kristy pointed. "There. See that? It's important."

Because he'd seen the movie before, he knew its importance, but had missed it the first time through. "How do you know?"

"The music changed and they focused on it too long."

"You're amazing." He kissed her temple. Any more than that and he wouldn't want to watch the movie, but that's what the evening was about. A taste of a date.

Every few minutes she commented on something happening in the movie. It gave a fuller experience, but he could understand how it might spoil it for some. He liked learning more about how her mind worked. None of the jobs she'd held had used anywhere near her potential. Her observation skills and ability to fit the clues together would make her a fine detective.

The closing credits began to roll.

Kristy tipped her head up. "Thank you. You didn't once cover my mouth or tell me to shut up."

"Oh, I can cover your mouth." He kissed her, being careful not to take it farther than he could handle. "I'd seen the movie before, but it was a whole new experience watching it with you."

She squinted. "Was this a good experience?"

"Oh, yeah. How about doing it again tomorrow night?"

Her grin told him how much it meant to her. It surged straight into his heart.

Chapter 8

A tapping in the library drew Mark's attention as he was steps from the kitchen. He peeked in and found Kristy diligently working at the table. She never got up before he did. He was amazed she could let this consume her the way it did—head down, tapping her pencil, and biting her lip. He would never have expected this determination about anything. His Kristy had unfathomed depths.

He thought he'd fallen for her eighteen months ago, but each day with her gave him a new insight, a new reason to love her. She was warmer, more willing to open up. She'd always held a piece of herself back, not letting go or letting him in. Seeing the relationship her parents had—one secretly cheating and pretending to love, and the other clueless—had to influence Kristy's outlook on relationships.

She'd changed, though. He attributed it to the therapist she'd mentioned. He'd subtly asked what was different with her, but she'd back off, change the subject, or rush off to do something else. He'd bide his time, demonstrate as best he could that she was the most important person in his world.

He grinned at her cute frown. She must have hit another dead end. He headed into the kitchen to make pancakes and bacon.

Once the food was cooked and in the oven to stay warm, he returned to the library to round up Kristy. He'd enjoyed how his dinner announcement had turned out, so he placed his hands in the same spot on the table. "Good Morning, beautiful."

Her fist jabbed her chest. "Mark! Don't do that to me."

"I love how you can concentrate so intently to the exclusion of anything else. Kind of how you make love."

"I'm surprised you can remember that, since it's been sooo…long."

He leaned closer, and tucked a strand of hair behind her ear. "Oh, I remember. Every touch. Every moan."

With the way her eyes softened, he could tell she was remembering, too.

He ran his hand through her strands. "Did I tell you how much I like your hair like this? It was nice before, but this is sexier."

She bit her lip. He wasn't used to seeing her unsure about the mention of sex.

He straightened with a snap. "Come on. I made breakfast."

"Ooh. Two meals in a row." Her eyes sparkled and she bounced out of her seat.

He waited for her to round the table and wrapped her in his arms. The kiss across the table had been nice, but this was where she should be. He kissed her, hoping he would have the strength to stop. She was his now more than ever before, but he still sensed a certain reserve. He peppered kisses along her jaw to her ear. "Let's go eat."

A moment of disappointment flashed across her face before she drew in a deep breath.

In the kitchen, Mark retrieved the hot plates and set them on the table. "Careful. It's hot."

"Duh."

He chuckled and poured coffee, then sat facing her. "What time did you get up?"

She poured syrup over her pancake. "Five. I had a dream about the cryptogram. I couldn't sleep after that. I had to try it out."

"And?" He shoved half a strip of bacon in his mouth.

"It broke my logjam. The rest should go faster."

"Great. One step closer to getting rid of these guys."

They finished their meal and Kristy returned to her puzzle.

Mark wished there was something productive he could do. He stuck his head into the library. "I'm going out to exercise."

Kristy grinned and started to rise.

He pointed a finger. "Stay there. No distractions."

"What do you mean?"

He leaned against the door opening. "I know you sit right there"—he pointed at the window seat—"and watch me exercise."

"You know I've watched you? It's better than hot guys on television." She fanned her face with her notepad. If he didn't have a plan, her dreamy expression would have him stripping them out of their clothes.

He stalked towards her, stopped beside her chair and lifted her chin with a finger. He gave her a kiss. "Why do you think I did a hundred push-ups instead of fifty? And I climbed that stupid wall to impress you."

She giggled. "Fine. I'll work the puzzle. But tomorrow, I'm watching you."

He couldn't resist giving her another kiss. "See you shortly." He liked that she found him hotter than the over-pumped guys on TV.

***

Although her thoughts kept straying to Mark, Kristy got

back to work on her cryptogram. She might as well be watching him, since she hadn't plugged in any letters since he left. She threw down her pencil and strode to the window, standing to the side instead of sitting, hoping he wouldn't notice her. Not all the course was visible from this position, but at the moment, Mark was.

He skirted to the side of the climbing wall and jumped on the balance beam. He really was serious when he said he climbed the wall for her. She didn't understand why he needed to impress her.

She couldn't figure him out. He might have thought being flirty with her made living in the same house easier for both of them. But it made her wonder if it meant he could leave without a backward glance. The only type of guy she understood was the one who wanted sex. And Mark wasn't that guy anymore.

Kristy hadn't seen her therapist in almost a year, but wished she could talk to her right now.

Mark disappeared from view as he neared the side of the house. She scurried back to the table. What happened to the concentration she was so good at?

She picked up her pencil and stared at the cryptogram pages. What she'd realized in her sleep was that five and seven letter words were reversed, but not any others like the last puzzle. She'd rewritten the cryptogram with the letter order correct, and it was falling into place more easily.

Footsteps caught her attention as Mark came in and sat at the desk, but she ignored them in hopes he would think she was deep into her work. Otherwise, he'd know she had spied on him. Not that it mattered.

The words filled in faster now. One missing letter only left so many choices and when compared to others using the same letter, most times it was obvious. She penciled in the last empty space and sat back. She scanned the lines and they all made sense, in a witchy sort of way. Most of it was a recipe, but the end was the beginning of the chant, or whatever the spoken words were called.

Kristy leaped to her feet. She pumped her fist in the air and did a hip wiggle. "Yes!"

"You solved it?" She'd forgotten that Mark had come in. His grin was infectious.

"Yes. The first—I mean—third one. The first two had the same key, so I hope three and four do. I can't believe I'm saying this, but I'm so done with this cryptogram."

"Because it's so hard?"

"No. I love the challenge. It's just taking so long, and I want this whole thing over with."

"I hope it's not because of me."

Her jaw dropped. She couldn't tell if he was teasing or actually believed it. She rushed across the room, and sat on the edge of the desk. "No. Not you. I'm glad we've spent this time together. It's because we need to stop these bad guys from doing bad things."

His face cleared, and he rolled his chair back, dragging her onto his lap. He buried his face in her shoulder and hugged her. It wasn't sexual, but she felt loved. Had she ever been hugged by a guy before in a way that didn't imply foreplay or sex?

She kissed his forehead like he sometimes did to her. It felt different. As if it was more important than all the other kisses that preceded it. It made no sense. How could lips to forehead mean more than deep kisses?

She wiggled out of his lap. "I better get back to work."

She tried to pull away, but he held her tighter. He gave her a short kiss. "When this is over, *we* aren't over. Got that? No more time limits."

She stared into his so serious brown eyes. "No more time limits."

He drew in a deep breath and let it out slowly, as if he'd accomplished something. "Okay. Go finish that puzzle."

She scampered back to the table, and called up the last cryptogram on her tablet. She wrote it down on a fresh sheet of paper, dropping the letter that didn't belong with what she now knew was the word 'a', and reversing the appropriate words. She hoped she didn't have to rewrite it because the key didn't work.

On the first line, she started the substitutions from her key. At the end of the line, she read through it. Yes! It worked. Within fifteen minutes, she had all the letters written down. She read the whole puzzle and all the words made sense. She grabbed the other solution, and read through from beginning to end. It was complete.

She wouldn't read it out loud. Ever. To make the spell work, the herbs and other ingredients would be mixed together, but she didn't want to take chances.

She jumped up with the sheets. "It's done."

She'd been too intent on the cryptogram to notice Mark had left. A glance at the wall clock showed it was afternoon. She wandered to the kitchen.

He glanced up from the sandwiches he was putting together. "Did you finish?"

She grinned and held the pages up. "Yes! Now you can send it to Jason."

"Great job, baby. I sure couldn't have done it." He picked up the two plates and headed to the kitchen table. "Let's eat, then I'll send it."

***

Mark sat across the kitchen table from Kristy. He'd insisted on cooking breakfast again this morning since she'd cooked so many dinners.

79

He'd hoped to hear from Jason the night before with the new solution, but nothing had come through. Shauna had insisted on sending it to Kathleen after they finished altering the spell, and the time difference in Britain probably accounted for the delay.

After Kristy pushed her plate away, he took her hand. "You seem calmer, not so antsy. We've been trapped in this house for over two weeks. When we were on the island, the only way I could get you to stay in our room was when we made love."

"I. Um. Feel better inside." She tapped her chest. "The therapist helped me to understand…me."

It took every bit of his willpower to resist taking her to bed, but he felt that their relationship would be stronger if she understood that she was the whole package for him. It wasn't just about sex. That's where they'd gone wrong last time. One of the ways. They probably hadn't said more than a dozen words to each other before having sex. Sure they'd had a lot of fun together after that, but he'd only realized how important she was shortly before she broke up with him. He hadn't had a chance to tell her, and was too angry to fight for her when she told him they were done.

He ran a finger down her cheek. "Can you tell me about it, so I can understand you better, too?"

Over the last couple weeks, he'd found out she was more complex than he ever expected. On first meeting her, he'd thought she was a spoiled only child, always getting what she wanted. Before the end of their time together, he realized she cared deeply for her father and Shauna.

She wrapped her hand around his. "I'm not sure I can. It's so personal. And there's more stuff I haven't even told Shauna."

He stood and drew her up. "I wouldn't tell anyone anything you told me. I just want to know you better so I don't screw up."

He steered her toward the door. She glanced over her shoulder. "The dishes—"

"I'll take care of them later."

This was the tricky part. He was being devious and underhanded, but the best way to get her to talk without falling apart and clamming up was to get her into the secret room. If she ever figured it out, he hoped she would forgive him.

"Let's go in the secret room, so we won't be disturbed or overheard in case Jason comes over."

She raised her brows. "I thought he'd just email you the altered solution. But okay."

Mark depressed the hidden button and swung the door open. He allowed Kristy to enter without touching her, so she wouldn't get zapped. He followed and closed the door. He rolled his head and shrugged his shoulders. That tingle was worse than last time.

Maybe someone was disapproving of his actions. But he was doing it for the best of reasons, and he didn't know if it would work. Maybe she was ready to tell him anyway.

Mark sat in the recliner and tugged Kristy onto his lap. He flipped up the foot rest and leaned the chair back. That's the way therapists did it, right? Lie on the couch, relax and tell your secrets. Maybe they didn't do it like that anymore. Whatever. It worked last time.

He kissed her forehead, and she snuggled closer.

"When did you see the therapist?"

"A couple of months after I broke up with you. Dad noticed I was…despondent. I couldn't talk about it because I'd have to tell him about the cheating. He found a friend of a friend who was a therapist and suggested I go. Why not? It might help. I probably should have gone as a teenager, but that would have meant Mom had to explain to Dad why I needed it and that wasn't going to happen."

"Over that guy you found her with in her bedroom?"

"No. She never found out I saw."

He felt gut punched. She got over that and there was something worse? "What happened to you when you were a teenager?"

She glanced at him and tucked herself back under his chin. "Do you remember what you got for your fifteenth birthday?"

That question was so out of left field, but he'd play along. "I think that was the year I got this tricked out bike I'd had my eye on for months."

Her head bumped his chin when she nodded. "Yeah. Pretty normal. After Dad got back from a mission, he gave me a beautiful dress he'd bought wherever he was. But Mom..."

The hesitation and lowered voice alerted him that he wouldn't like this.

"On the day of my fifteenth birthday, she took me to the doctor and got me a birth control prescription."

"Jeez." Parents should be protective of their little girls. He would be.

"I thought it was ridiculous. I hadn't even been kissed yet. But I took them because she kept reminding me. I wasn't planning on having sex anytime soon, but I guess she wanted to make sure I didn't make her a grandmother."

She unbuttoned and refastened a button on his shirt, over and over. He didn't think she even realized she was doing it.

"A few months later, I got home from visiting Shauna when Mom was leaving with this guy."

Mark didn't like where this was going. He didn't want to hear it, but what would happen if he stopped her now? He'd been the one to start this.

"A couple days later, he showed up just after I got home

from school."

He tensed, wondering if the man had raped her. If Mark could track the guy down, he'd kill him. Painfully. He worked at keeping anger out of his voice. "What happened?"

"He helped me with my Government homework. He worked somewhere in government and was so much more interesting than my teacher. When Mom arrived home, I was surprised when he told her he'd only been there a few minutes, and they left for their date."

"Then what happened?" He worked at relaxing his muscles, not wanting to project his anger.

"A few days later, he was waiting in his car when I got home from school. He helped me with homework again…and kissed me. Just on the cheek. But…"

"But what?" Mark imagined beating this predator who took advantage of a naïve girl.

Kristy clenched a fistful of his shirt. "Each time he visited, he pushed a little further. After the fourth visit, he wasn't helping with homework anymore."

"He seduced you?"

She bit her lip and stared at him. "Yeah, but I didn't know that's what it was at the time."

"That's statutory rape."

"I didn't know that either."

She dropped her head to his shoulder. "About a month later, Mom got home early on a night she didn't have a date with this guy. She caught us kissing in the living room. She blew her stack. Yelled at him that I was only fifteen and what did he think he was doing. I think she was more upset about that than losing her boyfriend, and I loved her for it. I never saw him again."

"That's it? Nothing happened to the guy?"

She shrugged. "Mom asked if he did more, and I told her no. I realized while she was yelling that what he did was wrong. But if I told her what he'd done, she'd go to the police about it, then Dad would find out this guy was Mom's boyfriend, and they'd divorce, and I would see Dad even less than I did. But what if I told Mom and she did nothing? Like I wasn't important enough to her. Either way, I'd lose."

"Honey, I'm so sorry." She'd had her innocence ripped from her, first by her mother and later by one of her mother's boyfriends.

She wiped a tear off her cheek. "I figured Mom intended for me to have sex with boys my own age and not men over thirty, so that's what I did." She sighed. "I was so messed up." She leaned back so her head rested on his arm and studied his face. "Do you hate me?"

"I love you. I could never hate you." He frowned. "Okay, to be totally honest, I hated you for about two weeks after you time limited me. But mostly I was hurt." He hadn't intended on telling her that, but apparently, the room was working on him, too.

"I'm sorry." She ran her fingers down his cheek and behind his neck. "We haven't had sex, so I thought you were still mad at me."

He blew out a long breath. "We've both had sex with a lot of people. At least for me, most of the time, it was fun and nothing more. With my job, I didn't think it would be fair to have a relationship."

He stared into her beautiful, intense eyes. "I want to show you that you're more important than that. I love being with you. I love your quirky personality. I love doing stuff with you. And because of all that, making love with you is fantastic."

She grinned. "So, when do we get to the fantastic part?"

He returned her grin. "When we're ready. Let's get out of here." He'd gotten what he wanted from the room—to understand Kristy better. But he so wished what she'd told him hadn't happened.

He set the chair upright, and stood with her still in his arms. He kissed her. Not one that led to getting naked, but hopefully, letting her know how important she was. "Once we get this crazy wizard stuff out of the way, I'll be glad it happened because it brought us back together."

"Me, too."

"Hold on." Mark put his hands on her back, holding her loose enough to see her face. "I want to thank you for talking to me."

She shrugged. "It actually felt kind of good telling you. When I told the therapist about it, there were all these emotional questions, and it stretched on and on. Once we were done, I was wiped, but lighter, too. I know I needed to talk about it, but I'd held onto it for so long." She kissed his cheek. "Thanks for understanding."

He nudged her toward the door, and stayed back a step as she stepped through. No sense having her experience the tingle. He shivered as he exited the room. Man, he hoped not to do that again.

"Hi, Jason," said Kristy. Well, that justified what he'd told her about using the room.

Mark sidestepped the door and shoved it closed. His friend sat at the desk, his phone in one hand and a smirk on his face.

Mark pointed behind him. "We only talked in there." Jason lifted a brow, and Mark wished he hadn't said anything. "What brings you here, bro?"

"Shauna and I finished rewriting the spell. We got Mom's approval this morning. She made some alterations, so we're good to go." A sheet of paper sat on the desk.

"Good. How do we know when they try to use it? I'm sure it won't be immediate, since they'll have to gather the ingredients."

Jason shrugged. "We left the ingredients to Mom since she knows more about that. She said she put in one that's kind of rare, so it might take them longer to find it."

"If they were all common, we could get this done faster. The original didn't have it, did it?"

"Nah. It had something else rare that she substituted. She thought it would seem more real if they weren't all common ingredients."

Mark propped a hip on the desk, pulled Kristy into him, and ignored Jason's questioning expression. Mark had come a long way from 'get me out of here'. "Do we have to continuously monitor?"

"No. The spell will leave a residue, but it will fade. You don't want to leave it too long. Probably checking every two hours will be good enough." He withdrew from his pocket a two inch long brass pendulum, big on top and pointed on the bottom, and dangling from a chain. "I'm working and Shauna's got the baby, so I figured you two can take care of this part."

Jason's gaze turned to Kristy. "Can you get your tablet?"

"Sure." She scooped her tablet up from the library table. Before turning it over to Jason, she entered the password. That password had been the first indication that there was still something between them. He was glad it happened.

Jason typed in the electronic keyboard. "I hate tablets." A map of the United States appeared in a browser window. He set the tablet flat on the desk, and held the pendulum over the center. "Hold it like this, in the middle, about a half-inch from the screen."

Mark chuckled. "Boy, that's mixing old magic with new technology. Is this going to work for us? We don't have…abilities."

"Yes. Mom helped us write the spell for the pendulum, so anybody can use it." His friend grinned at Mark. "Even powerless people like you."

Jason dropped the pendulum into Kristy's outstretched hand. "Oh, and as it chooses a spot, enlarge that part of the map. Keep doing it until you've got it hovering over a specific building."

Mark clapped a hand on Jason's shoulder. "Great. This would have been impossible with paper maps."

"Harder, but not impossible." Jason stood. "I've got to get back to work. Let me know when something turns up."

His gaze followed Jason until the door closed behind him. Kristy set the pendulum on the desk and faced Mark. "The sooner I get the solutions sent in, the faster we can find these guys' location."

Chapter 9

Kristy stood beside the desk and gripped Mark's hand. "Do you want to do this?"

"Go ahead. It's your cryptogram."

"Okay." She picked up the pendulum. It had been only three hours since she typed the solution into the fake website, and it wasn't likely the bad guys had seen it and put together the ingredients, but they had to make sure. They didn't know how fast the locator in the spell would fade, and couldn't take any chances.

She held the weight over the map on her tablet and waited for it to stop swinging or do something weird. After a half minute, it stilled.

She glanced at Mark. "I don't think they've tried it yet, unless you think they're in the middle of Kansas."

"Yeah, it's pretty unlikely that the place that's straight under the pendulum is it."

"Just to make sure, I'll move it and see if it draws back to the same spot." She had no idea how the pendulum was supposed to react to the spell. She shifted it left an inch. Once it stopped moving, Colorado was the new favorite.

She set the weight beside her tablet. "I guess we try again."

Mark took out his phone. "I'm setting a two-hour timer."

Kristy rubbed her shoulders. "Are we going to have to

wake up every two hours through the night? Jeez. It's like a newborn baby."

Mark chuckled. "No. I'll check once in the night. That should be good." He took her hand. "Come on. I want to talk."

She squeezed his hand reflexively. "Is this bad?"

"No."

"Good. Let's sit in the window."

He glanced at the window and down his long legs. "I don't think I'll fit."

She dragged him across the room. "Sure you will. I do puzzles. I know how to make things fit."

"Yeah. Like a pretzel."

She giggled and pushed him onto the seat. "Now turn so your back is mostly against the side wall and pull up this leg." She touched his left one. "Leave the other on the floor." She patted the triangle between his legs. "Now, there's my spot."

She clambered up and dropped her butt into the space, her feet on the other side of his drawn up leg, and her shoulder against his chest. She gazed into his face. "See. Perfect."

"Perfect like half a pretzel." He tipped her head up with the side of his finger and kissed her. "After we bag these guys, I want you to meet my family."

The breath in her lungs stopped moving. No guy had ever, *ever* wanted her to meet his family. In some cases, she was pretty sure she'd been a guilty pleasure—maybe more than some. Not that she'd been with any men who were married. At least she hoped not. She couldn't say if there'd been any engaged men. Some guys were scum.

"I-I'd like that." He'd already met her family—he worked with her dad, and he knew Shauna, of course.

"Mom's fiftieth birthday is in a month, and I want you

there for her party."

Maybe that would work nicely. She could get a little dose of his family at the gathering.

"It's just for family. Dad, my sister and her family, my brother, cousins, aunts and uncle, Mom's best friend. Lots of kids. About thirty people."

"I didn't even know you had a sister until that dinner at Shauna's. Now, there're all these other family members." She'd be trapped with a bunch of people Mark knew, and she didn't. A couple of years ago that would have been fine. She could work her way through a crowd by flirting. That wouldn't work with the new Kristy and Mark's family. But maybe she could get them to reveal some secrets about Mark.

"That was another mistake of LBTL."

She frowned. "What?"

"Life Before Time Limit. I didn't treat our time together as a real relationship. I didn't tell you personal things about myself."

She grinned and kissed his jaw. They were both working harder at it this time, both more committed. She leaned into him. "Okay. Tell me about your family."

He wrapped his arms around her. "My parents had their thirtieth anniversary about six months ago."

"Are they still happy together?"

"Yes. They spent months planning a three-week trip as an anniversary gift to each other. They visited some of the places we'd vacationed as I was growing up and added a few days at *Pirates' Cove*."

She twisted around. "You told them about *Pirates' Cove*?"

"I have good memories there. And it's a beautiful place." He grinned. "I had to dodge questions about what I did there and who I was with."

"I have good memories, too." She settled back into his

embrace.

"My brother, Dennis, is two years younger than me, and way smarter, but don't tell him I said that. He works for one of the big banks in computer security. My sister, Wendy, is married to a guy she met in college. He's from China. He's doing solar research, and she's been assisting him for about a year."

"What are the twins' names?"

A silent chuckle shook his chest. "Don't laugh. Tabby and Sammy."

She squinted at him. "What do you…Oh, my god. Tabitha and Samantha from the old TV show *Bewitched*?"

"The same. She's obsessed."

"I bet she didn't tell her husband where she found the names."

"Oh, he knows. But he loves her."

She clasped his hand. "I can't believe this. Your sister loves a show about witches, and your best friend happens to have witchy abilities."

His chin rubbed against her head. "Sometimes I've been so tempted to tell her, but no. She doesn't know."

They'd missed this the first time around—really getting to know each other. It had been a silent agreement to keep things light, not reveal too much.

She twisted around and slid her hands behind his neck. Her heart pounded. This was the most important moment of her life, and she hoped she didn't screw it up. She stared into his compassionate eyes, building up her courage—not something she usually had to work at. "The only people I've ever said this to are my father and Shauna."

His eyebrows shot up.

"I love you."

His leg swung around so his foot dropped to the floor. She now sat on his lap, and he kissed her, long and hard. He nibbled kisses along her cheek to her ear. "I feel like I've been waiting forever for you to say that. Want to go up to my room?"

She leaned back. "Really? That's all it took?"

"All! Baby, that's everything. I had lots of indications you loved me, but I wasn't sure if you were committed to us"—he tapped her bottom lip with a finger—"until the words passed those beautiful lips."

He scooped an arm under her knees and stood. She tightened her hold around the back of his neck. "You can't carry me upstairs."

He took long strides through the room. "Sure, I can. Why do you think I've been doing all those exercises?"

"To keep strong?"

"Yeah. Strong enough to carry you wherever I need to."

Kristy laughed and kissed his neck. She'd gotten used to her celibate life, until Mark had crashed back into it. It had been easy to ignore all those pretty male bodies and turn down offers of fun when there was only one man she wanted. Two years ago, if someone had told her she'd go a month without sex, she would have laughed in their face. And now it had been eighteen months.

The dry spell was about to end in the best possible way. Kristy flicked Mark's earlobe with her tongue.

His arms tightened around her, and he paused with his foot on the first step. "Woman, if you don't want me to drop you, you'll stop that."

"You won't drop me." To prove she trusted him, she did it again, then kissed his neck. She slipped one hand down his chest, wishing he had a button-down shirt on instead of a t-shirt. She skimmed her hand across his chest until she reached his nipple, and rubbed her thumb over it. Liking so much how he sucked in a breath, she did it again.

His footsteps pounded up the stairs. He turned into the

first room and kicked the door closed. At the bed, he released her knees, and she slid down his body.

He held her head between his hands and kissed her. "I want you naked."

"Me, too. You."

Mark chuckled and yanked his shirt over his head. She hesitated with her hands on the bottom of her shirt, a new experience for her. By the time they got to the bedroom, normally she'd be committed to the act. Kristy was afraid having sex now would change how he felt about her. They'd been good together before, but it had been superficial. The closeness and sharing they'd achieved could be lost. But boy, she wanted to do this.

He tipped up her chin. "Hey, what's wrong?"

"I don't want to go back to the way we were before I broke up with you because we have sex."

He wrapped his arms around her. "We're about to make love. And it will be better than before because our relationship is better. We won't lose what we've built up."

He lifted her shirt, and she raised her arms, letting him remove it. He ran a finger along the edge of her bra. "That outfit you had on yesterday drove me crazy. Where did it come from?"

"Shauna brought it. I couldn't tell you were affected."

He kissed her neck. "Oh, I was. I can't imagine Shauna owning clothes like that."

Kristy giggled. "She wouldn't. I haven't worn club clothes in so long, and I didn't pack any, so Shauna bought them."

Mark unclipped her bra. She dropped her hands and it fell to the floor.

"I'll have to thank her."

His fingers brushed her stomach, freeing the button on her pants, and sliding the zipper down.

"I think she might be embarrassed if you do."

His warm, slightly rough hands snuck into her pants and slid them off her hips. "That's the chance she took when she bought them."

Kristy had enough of being passive. That's not how sex worked with her. Ever. She unbuckled his belt, popped the button, and dragged the zipper pull down. She released him and pushed the pants to his knees. He kicked out of them and scooped her up, laying her on the bed. The rest of her clothes disappeared.

His glorious body covered hers, and he kissed her. She ran her hands up his muscled arms and over his bulging shoulders. It seemed impossible that his body was more beautiful than before.

He feathered kisses over the corners of her mouth. "I missed you so much."

"You better prove it. I think my body forgot what an orgasm feels like."

He chuckled. "I'll get right on that." He nibbled her neck, and she shivered.

It was almost a dream. She never thought they'd share a bed again. It was the same yet different from the other times they'd been together. She no longer felt she had to give to get the attention she wanted. Her focus had changed. She would give Mark every pleasure she could think of because she wanted that for him. This time, her goal wasn't her own satisfaction.

Mark's lips nuzzled her breast, and she lightly scraped her nails across his scalp. She squeezed the back of his neck, then ran her hands down his back, over the ridged muscles. He slipped lower and his mouth devoured her. She buried her hands in his hair, and moaned. In record time, ripples overtook her, and she clenched her hands in his hair.

Mark rose up, taking her mouth in a searing kiss. She

nudged his shoulder, and he raised his eyebrows, staring at her.

"Roll over."

He dropped to his shoulder to lie beside her, but she kept a tight hold and rolled with him until he was on his back with her on top of him. "This is where I want you." She kissed him and let her fingers explore as she worked her way down his body. She rained kisses on his chest before heading lower. Her hand found him first, and she caressed his firm flesh before giving a kiss. Her mouth took him in.

"No-no-no." His voice was a lust filled whisper.

He grabbed her under the arms and dragged her up, kissing her as he entered her warmth. Kristy didn't know how long it took, but every movement, every kiss, everywhere his hands touched drove her higher and higher. She buried her face in his neck as her body exploded in sensation. Mark moaned and drew her closer.

She'd become a splat of boneless body scattered across Mark's torso. She enjoyed rising and falling as he took each breath, knowing that she'd affected him as much as he had her. Maybe she had forgotten what an orgasm felt like, because this one was like no other she'd ever experienced.

Kristy struggled, but managed to lift her head to stare into Mark's face. "That was..." She wet her lips. "That was amazing. I think...it was the first time I ever felt like...I made love."

He grinned and placed a palm on each side of her head, stretched his neck and kissed her. He dropped his head back down but rubbed her cheeks with his thumbs. "It won't be the last. I love you."

She buried her face in his neck and ran her hand up and down his muscled arm. She never, ever expected to feel this good again. No, it wasn't again. She'd never felt this good. Even when she'd been with Mark before, she knew it would end. Either he'd get tired of her, or she'd get tired of him, or she'd screw up. It had never felt real. She'd been happy, but in-a-dream kind of happy. This was real.

Tears filled her eyes. She didn't cry. She blinked to stop them. It didn't help.

"Hey, are you drooling on me?"

She tried to laugh, but a sob escaped.

Mark rolled them to their sides and leaned back. He swiped a tear. "What's this?"

"I don't know." She dragged in a breath, let it out slowly, and stared into those gorgeous warm brown eyes. "I never thought I'd see you again. But you're real. We're real."

His lips grazed her wet cheek. "We *are* real. More real than last time." He studied her as if he was assessing her. He patted her shoulder. "I have something for you."

He got out of bed and opened the closet. A loud zipper rasped. He returned to the bed and sat beside her. She pushed up and curled her legs under her.

He stared at his closed hand. "I don't know why I stuck this in my bag at the last moment."

His gaze met hers and her breath caught. Love, and longing and worry reached out to her.

Mark brushed a strand of her beautiful hair behind her ear. "Somehow I knew something would be different between us. Being trapped in here together, we couldn't have regular dates, but I was determined that we got to know each other better before going to bed." He grinned. "Sometimes you made that really hard. But I persevered because I knew we needed a better foundation this time."

He lifted his hand to chest height and opened it. A ring rested on his palm. His gaze swept over her face and his voice was almost a whisper. "Kristy, will you marry me?"

This time she didn't try to hold back the tears. Her life had turned around in weeks. Where she'd been lonely and heartbroken, Mark had filled her heart and mended it.

"Yes." She lunged for him and he tumbled backwards with a laugh.

He plucked her hand from his shoulder. "Here let me get this on you before we lose it." He slipped the ring on her finger and kissed her knuckle. "There. Now it's sealed in place."

She hadn't examined the ring. Now, she held her hand up and studied the symbol of their love. The center diamond was just the right size surrounded by three smaller ones on each side, forming a triangle. "It's beautiful." She squinted. "How do you happen to have this?"

He sat up, taking her with him and gazed at her for several moments. "I bought it two days before you broke up with me."

She thought she was done with tears, but more found their way down her cheeks. "I'm so sorry."

"We needed the break. Otherwise, you wouldn't have seen that therapist who helped you so much."

As if *they'd* broken up. It was all her. And she loved him more for not laying the blame just on her.

He caressed her jaw with his thumb. "And I might not have understood if some crazy stuff happened without knowing how your past affected you."

"I don't deserve you."

He shook his head. "Baby, I'm not perfect. Just remember that." Mark stood. "Let's get dressed and check if the spell's been used."

She'd totally forgotten the danger they still faced. He'd try harder than ever to keep her safe, but she didn't want him risking his life for her.

Chapter 10

Mark had expected a test of the solved spell within twenty-four hours, but three days had passed since they sent it out. He was relieved Reese and Kathleen Ballard had come across some interesting research and extended their stay in England, so he and Kristy wouldn't have to vacate the house. He'd rather be a stone's throw from Jason than a hundred miles away in a safe house where he'd have no backup.

He sat at the library desk and sipped his coffee. Kristy had pushed him out of the kitchen while she cleaned after breakfast. She had used the locator pendulum every two hours while they were both awake. In the night, he'd get up and give it a go, but so far, nothing. He was beginning to think the spell didn't work.

He laced his hands behind his head and grinned. Getting up around two in the morning wasn't his idea of fun, but after he'd done the chore and crawled back into bed, Kristy made it worthwhile. That first night, he hadn't expected she'd be awake, but she said it woke her when she didn't find him to wrap herself around. Of course, they made love and the following nights as well.

Kristy stopped in the doorway. "What's that silly grin for?"

His grinned widened. "Just thinking about our two a.m. trysts."

She flew across the room and kissed him. "And all those other times?"

"Every single one." He dragged the tablet and pendulum closer. "Want to do the honors?"

She tapped the screen, entered her password, and picked up the pendulum. "This isn't exciting anymore. Maybe the spell is broken."

"My thought, too, but we don't have anything else we can do right now."

The weight swung lazily over the electronic map, and as always, lost momentum and settled straight down, over whatever area of the map she held it above.

Kristy sighed and set the pendulum on the desk. She stepped behind his chair and wrapped her arms around his shoulders. He couldn't believe how quickly they'd gotten comfortable touching, holding, and talking. It was as if all the time between their breakup and now had disappeared. Only this time, it was better, deeper.

He tipped his head back and studied her. "Have you checked your email recently? If they tried the spell and our locator isn't working, they might have sent you something about it."

She moved to his side and opened her email program. "I haven't looked in a few days." She scrolled through her messages. "No. Nothing from them, but here's one from Dad."

She clicked on it, and he read beside her.

"Whoa! They're getting married in five weeks." She stared at him with panic in her eyes. "This will be cleared up by then, won't it?"

"I would hope so, but you're going no matter what." He wrapped an arm around her. No way would he let her miss the wedding of the man who'd been the most important person in her life. At least until now.

He patted her hip and released her. "Okay. Be back here in two hours."

She shook her head. "You say that as if I'm going to go shopping or something."

He chuckled.

She pointed a finger at him. "Just for that, the first chance I get, you're coming with me. We'll shop for a wedding present and a dress."

He grabbed her finger and gently bit the tip. "Do I get to go in the changing room with you?"

"You're impossible." She snatched her tablet and stalked to the table where she picked up her notepad and pencil, then climbed onto the window seat.

Mark opened his laptop and worked on some business for Jack. The man had been surprised when Mark had refused an away mission but accepted the research job. A far cry from 'send me on the next job.' Now, he needed to make sure Jack didn't find out that Mark was protecting his daughter, and a whole lot more. He wasn't sure how Jack would react to finding out Kristy was in danger over some crazy witchcraft spells.

"Kristy, you ready to try again?" He could have gone ahead and done the locating most of the time, but she'd sort of fixated on it since she blamed herself for causing the trouble.

"Already?" She set her notebook, along with the pencil on the seat and joined him with the tablet. "Scoot."

He stood and let her take the chair. He dropped his hand on her shoulder and kissed her temple. He didn't know how he'd survived being without her for so long. He lifted her left hand and kissed her ring. "How did Shauna take it when you told her we're engaged?"

She giggled. "I haven't told her yet. I want to have them over for dinner again and see how long it takes her to notice this." She wiggled her fingers.

"I have a feeling she'll be mad that you waited to tell her."

She giggled again. "I know. But she'll be so excited for me that she'll get over it fast."

Kristy switched the tablet screen to a U.S. map and picked up the pendulum. She held it over the center and it swung in a circle, then veered east. "Oh, wow. It's pulling." She shifted her hand more in that direction and the pendulum settled over the northeastern states. "It's tugging down like it wants to touch the map."

"Let's enlarge that section."

She used a finger to center the spot on the map and expanded it with her finger and thumb. She trembled under his hand as she lifted the pendulum back in place.

"Stay steady."

The pendulum swung in a circle before tugging east again. Kristy centered the area and expanded it, revealing parts of Connecticut, New York and Pennsylvania. The weight swung and selected its spot.

She shifted the map again. "It's New York or Pennsylvania."

The pendulum chose another spot, and Kristy adjusted the map. "White Plains."

The map was zoomed enough to show major highways, and she narrowed down to near Interstate 287. A couple more adjustments and she hovered over a building. "Gotcha."

She dropped the pendulum, jumped up and, hugged and kissed Mark. "I didn't think this would work."

"One step closer, baby." He typed the address into his phone, leaned a hip against the desk, then called Jason.

"Hey. What's up?"

"We've got an address."

"It worked?"

Mark shook his head. "How come you sound surprised? You're the one who thought of this."

"Not every spell works the way it's planned or someone does it wrong. So, where is it?"

"White Plains, New York."

"That's not too far."

Kristy tapped Mark's arm and pointed to the screen. She'd mapped directions.

"It's about two-and-a-half hours."

"Let's do a recon. Say we leave in about an hour?"

Mark rubbed his temples. "First off, I'm not leaving Kristy here alone."

She grinned.

"And she's not coming with us."

Her expression turned to a pout.

"I can't risk her coming to my house," Jason said.

Mark didn't want to put Shauna and Logan in harm's way, either.

"I got it," Jason said. "My new guy who started last week is ex-military. I can take him off his assignment and have him stay with Kristy."

"Do you trust him enough to protect her?"

"Yes. He was assigned to protect dignitaries visiting Iraq."

Mark didn't want to trust someone he hadn't met, but they'd been in limbo too long. Jason trusted the man, but Mark wished Jason had worked with him longer. "All right. Bring him in. In the meantime, I want to do some research on this building before leaving. We'll leave in two hours."

"Got it. I'll have him follow me over when I come to pick you up."

Mark swiped his phone and set it on his desk. He took Kristy's hand. "I don't like this."

She ran her hand up and down his arm. "But this is what

we've been waiting for."

He gave a dry chuckle. "Yeah. Me, the great mission planner, didn't even think through how we were going after these guys and protect you at the same time."

He tipped her head up so he could peer into her eyes. "Stay in the hidden room while we're gone."

Her eyes widened, and she jabbed his shoulder. "Seriously? It's a five-hour drive round trip, on top of however long you're there. That could be eight hours. I do need to eat and use a bathroom."

"You could—"

She pointed a finger at him. "Don't you dare say I can use some kind of makeshift chamber pot. It's not happening."

He chuckled. "I bet if you checked in the attic, you could find a real one."

"Grrr. You are impossible."

He loved this side of Kristy—getting her all riled up.

He bracketed her face in his hands and kissed her. "I'm worried about you. How about if you take all the food in there with you that you'll need for eight hours and only come out twice to use the bathroom?" He'd rather go with the chamber pot idea but saw her point.

"All right."

"And we'll post Jason's guy right here." He patted the armrest. "Unless you want him inside with you."

She shook her head. "No. Out here. I don't want to try to entertain him for hours on end."

"Good. I want to be the only guy you entertain."

She narrowed her eyes. "Men and women can entertain each other in ways besides having sex. Can't they?" She closed her eyes. "Jeez. I don't even know."

He pulled her to her feet and hugged her. He would have laughed, except this was another way her mother had messed her up. Kristy hadn't had normal teen dates that might have ended without a kiss, or participated with groups of kids having fun together. Their first time around, he hadn't been much better. They'd spent time on the beach, snorkeled and rented a boat, but it had been mostly sex. This time, they'd have lots of activities outside the bedroom.

He tapped her hip. "Go make your meals. I have some research to do."

She left the room and he immediately missed her warmth. He had to leave her to wrap this up, but he didn't feel good about it.

***

Mark popped the last bite of the sandwich Kristy made into his mouth. Seconds later, Jason came through the front door, followed by a man in black jeans and navy t-shirt. About four inches shorter than Jason, the guy had black hair and skin the color of coffee with cream.

Mark met them at the library doors, and held out his hand. "Mark Simmons."

The man accepted. "Ward Cordero." He smiled, accentuating a one-inch scar on his chin. Hopefully, that meant he'd seen some kind of action. Seeing the gun in a well worn holster under his jacket helped, too.

Kristy came out of the kitchen and wrapped an arm around Mark's waist. He dropped his over her shoulders. "Kristy, this is Ward. He's in charge of your safety, so if he tells you to do something, you'd better do it."

Her mouth thinned. "I know. Jason, did you get lunch? I can make a sandwich. What about you, Ward?"

"I already ate. Thanks, Kristy," Jason said.

"I'm all set, ma'am."

Kristy's eyebrows shot up. "Ma'am? Seriously? You better not be thinking that I'm lots older than you. Don't ma'am me."

Ward chuckled. "Sorry...Kristy. It won't happen again."

Mark squeezed her shoulder. "Why don't you go use the bathroom while we're still here?"

She glared. "Yeah. I'll get right on that, Dad." She stalked to the kitchen.

Ward grinned. "She seems quite the handful."

"She's worth it."

Jason didn't quite hide a chuckle by clearing his throat. "I'm glad this forced arrangement has worked out."

"Me, too. Anyway, Ward, Kristy has opted to stay alone in the safe room, and you can sit in the library." He pointed at the desk. "I find that's the best place to see the front door, and you're only steps away from where Kristy will be. She's promised to only come out a couple of times while we're gone for bathroom breaks. Feel free to raid the kitchen."

Kristy returned with a paper grocery bag in her arms. Mark took it from her, surprised how heavy it was. He peeked inside. "Jeez. What do you have in here? It must be enough food for two days."

She ticked off on her fingers. "There's my dinner, and snacks for this afternoon and tonight. I added breakfast, just in case. And drinks."

"Okay. I'll walk you to your hideout."

She raised her brows. "Bye, guys." She headed to the room.

"Don't forget your tablet."

"Oh, thanks." She detoured to the desk and retrieved it. At the door to the secret room, she pushed the button to open it and stepped through.

Behind him, Ward spoke. "Wow. I didn't expect that."

Mark was glad his body blocked how Kristy had opened the door. He followed her and set the bag on the table. He didn't even mind the shiver of the spell since he'd get Kristy alone for one more minute. He pushed her up against the wall. "I'll miss you."

She looped her arms around his neck. "Me, too. Be careful. And thank you."

"I'll do everything I can to keep you safe. We'll be back as soon as we can." He kissed her. He didn't want to leave. He had a bad feeling about the whole mission. He stepped back and touched her cheek. "You be careful, too."

He exited, shoved the door closed, and joined Jason in the foyer. "Ready?"

"Yes." At the front door, Jason turned back. "Ward, throw the deadbolt."

"Yes, sir."

Mark paused outside until the lock clicked into place, then transferred a backpack from the back of his SUV to Jason's backseat, and got into the passenger side of Jason's vehicle. He set his phone into the holder. "I already mapped the address."

Jason backed onto the street. "What did you find?"

Mark slid the seat back several notches. "Nothing useful. It sounds like a legit company. Freeland Enterprises. They invest in small companies, offer advice for growth, and after five years, either sell back their interests to the company or to someone else for a tidy profit."

Jason glanced at him. "You checked into some of the companies they invested in?"

"Yes. All the ones they listed on their website did really well—while they owned shares and afterward."

"Too bad you can't find a list of companies they bought into that didn't do as well."

Mark rubbed his temples with fingers and thumb. "I'd have to break through their security to find it, and I didn't have the time. We'll search for that in the building if we get the chance. And on the way there, I'll research the executives. Not that I'll get any secret information through my phone." He wished he had at least a full day for research, but they had to jump in since these guys would have figured out that the spell was a bust. He had no idea what their reaction would be.

Jason hit the turn signal and entered the highway. "What's the plan?"

"We're getting there in daylight, so we'll park a couple of blocks away and hoof it back. We'll circle at the edge of the property, check for any other exits. I brought binoculars to search for activity through the windows."

"And after dark?"

"We'll wait until everybody, or almost everybody, leaves and have a peek inside. Maybe the executives' offices will reveal why they want the spell."

Jason cracked a bottle of water and took a swig then deposited the bottle in its holder. "So..."

Mark wouldn't respond to that. Whenever Jason started that way and paused it was something Mark didn't want to discuss.

It must have been a full minute before Jason spoke again. "You and Kristy officially back together?"

At least that one was easy. "Yes." Mark kept his eyes glued to the road ahead.

"You two worked out whatever caused you to breakup?"

Mark blew out a long breath. "Yes. Can we be done talking about this?"

Jason slanted a glance to Mark. "I just want to make sure you know what you're doing with Kristy. You were kind of a mess for a while last time."

Mark glared. "And you figured you'd throw me into it again?"

Jason ran a hand through his hair. "Actually, I was thinking that I wanted to keep Shauna's best friend safe.

Sorry. But it seems to be working out."

Mark closed his eyes and tipped his head back. "Now. But there for a while, it was the pits." It was nice his friend cared about him, but the only one he wanted to talk about it with was Kristy.

"So—"

"End of discussion." Mark turned on the radio, his thoughts on Kristy. The farther he got from her, the more he worried he might never see her again.

Chapter 11

As Jason slowed while passing the two-story Freeland Enterprises building, Mark's gaze darted over the property. He didn't see security cameras. A wide expanse of grass lined both sides. A swath of lawn and a few shrubs landscaped the front. A sidewalk bordered the parking area. A couple dozen cars parked along the walk and the spaces closer to the road.

Along the right side, a bordering of sparse woods separated the building from its neighbor. As far as Mark could see behind, grass led to more woods. The far side of the structure, a parking lot on the neighboring property made it impossible to observe from there.

About a half-mile up, Jason parked on the side of the road behind a pickup truck. Lucky for them, they'd found a path into the woods with a sign proclaiming *Whitman's Forest*. They checked their ammo and shoved their guns back into the holsters under their jackets. Mark activated a tracking app on his phone. If needed, they'd be able to find the path later in the dark.

They exited the vehicle and shouldered their backpacks. To the average person, they'd resemble two over-prepared hikers.

A short way in, another path bisected theirs, and Mark turned right. A man and woman approached, and the two men stepped off the trail. Mark gave a nod.

The couple stopped, and the man spoke. "Are you going to the pond?"

Mark dropped into hiker mode. "That was our plan."

"When we left, a doe and fawn were at the water, so if you go in quiet, you might still see them."

Mark grinned. "Thanks, man. Good to know."

After the couple's footsteps faded, Jason asked, "You going fishing?"

"Only if we have bait for bad guys."

His friend chuckled. He and Jason had been on more missions together than he could remember. They'd saved each other's lives a few times, enough that Mark didn't know who owed whom. Jason would always be Mark's first pick to have at his back.

Five minutes later, Mark found a narrow path to the right. It should lead to their target building. He stopped a few feet back from the edge of the woods.

Jason stepped beside him. "There it is. Let's get off the trail and see what's of interest through the windows."

Mark worked his way through underbrush, snagging a pant leg on briars, and stopped behind a tree with a wide trunk near the grass. He swung his backpack down and fished out his binoculars from a side pocket. Eight feet away, Jason did the same.

Through the lenses, Mark inspected the back of the building. Solid, gray doors with no doorknobs were set about ten feet from each end of the building—probably fire exits. He still couldn't find any security cameras. They should have some kind of precautions in place, and it worried him that they might be supernatural. As on the front, two horizontal ribbons of windows spanned the back wall. He worked his way across the first floor windows, stopping at each one for a few seconds before moving on. Some people moved about, and others were positioned lower, probably sitting at desks, but most views were of walls, doors or door openings.

His scan of the second floor was less revealing. Except for one man standing close to a window with his back to it, all he saw were ceilings.

He stuffed his binoculars back into his pack. "Let's head to the side of the building and find a better view."

"Sure."

Mark followed the small path to the main one and took a right. He paced off the distance that should take him past the building and lawn, and a bit farther. No convenient path. A giant step over a patch of brambles landed him in a small clearing. He worked his way perpendicular to the path, zigzagging between trees and over fallen trunks. He hoped nobody from the building was outside since he and Jason rustled leaves and snapped dead branches.

Soon, the building was visible through the trees, and Mark angled to center on it. He found a wide tree to hide behind, and Jason picked one nearby. Mark scanned the second-floor windows, not finding anything, then started on the first-floor, slowly viewing each window. A movement caught his eye, and he zoomed in. A woman in a business suit strode through a doorway carrying a file folder. A man followed her. She half-turned and said something over her shoulder. The door closed, and a few steps in, the man grabbed her arm and spun her to face him.

"Son of a bitch!" he said in a hoarse whisper.

"What?"

Mark didn't shift his eyes from the room. "Fourth window from the right. That's the man I had arrested who escaped." They were definitely in the right place.

The man crowded the woman and jerked his head as he spoke. He raised his hand, and she turned her head to the side. He pinched her chin and twisted her face back to him.

He ground his lips onto hers, and she punched his shoulder with the heel of her hand.

Jason swore. "I wish I was in there. I'd make him pay for that."

There was nothing they could do. They'd be stopped by security if they ran through the front door. Someone was bound to recognize him.

The woman must have bit the man. He backed away and rubbed a hand over his bloody mouth.

"Good for her," Jason said.

"Seriously? You think she's better off now than before?"

Jason let out a long breath. "Probably not."

The man shook a finger at the woman and stormed from the room. The woman's arms stiffened as if leaning on the desk, and bowed her head. Mark stayed focused on that room. A woman with enough courage to bite a man attacking her wouldn't stay down for long. She tossed her head back, then sat in a high-backed chair. A couple of minutes later, she slung a purse strap over her shoulder.

Mark stuffed his binoculars into his bag and swung it over his shoulder. "She's leaving. Let's try to talk to her."

Jason shook his head. "She was just accosted by a man. Do you think she's going to talk to two guys running up to her?"

"Probably not, but I've got to try." This could lead to a way to protect Kristy. Mark broke out onto the lawn. He kept an eye on the windows, but didn't see anyone peering out. He ran along the tree line until hitting the road, then ran along the edge of it to the driveway.

He stopped beside the sign for the business and watched the door. The woman they'd seen through the window strode out and traipsed between cars. Once he figured out which car she was headed toward, he met her beside it. Up close, she was a beautiful woman—shiny, black hair in a short, no nonsense cut.

He hated the fear in her brown eyes, and held his hands up in peace, keeping his back to the building. If that man followed her, he didn't want to be recognized. "I need your help." He'd go for it. "I was spying through the windows and saw that man attack you."

Her eyes widened, and she shifted her purse between them, but she didn't open her door.

"He tried to kidnap my fiancée, and I need to stop him from trying again. I hope you can help me."

She glanced at the building. "I don't know what I can do. I have my own trouble." She reached for the door handle.

He waved at her car. "Please. Maybe we can help each other. Can I get in with you, and we'll leave?" He glanced at Jason, standing at the road.

The woman's gaze darted to Jason. "What about him?"

"He can follow us. My fiancée is his wife's best friend."

She stared at his backpack. Maybe she worried about the contents.

"Jason, catch." He tossed his bag, and Jason took a step closer to catch it.

She let out a sigh and studied his face. "All right." The door locks clicked.

"Jason, get the car and follow."

"By the way, I'm Mark Simmons. He's Jason Ballard."

"I'm Sheila Michaels."

He raced around the car and got inside before she changed her mind. A quick glance didn't find anyone watching.

She backed out of her space, and got on the road, turning left.

"How about we go to a coffee shop and talk?"

"All right, but—I have to pick my daughter up in an hour."

Mark pulled his phone out and turned off the tracking app and shot Jason a text that they were going for coffee. He pointed his thumb back the way they'd come. "Who is that guy?"

"Head of security. Brother-in-law of one of the owners. Carl Gretsky."

"Has he always been like that?"

Her fingers tightened on the steering wheel. "He's been coming onto me since I started working there. He'd touch me and get too close. Try to talk me into going out with him. He gives me the creeps. What happened today, he's never done before."

She turned into a lot for a donut shop and parked near the door. Jason parked a couple of spaces down. They entered, and she strode to the counter and ordered. He added his and Jason's coffees and paid the bill.

She led them to a table near the wall. Mark steered her to a seat where she faced the wall. He didn't want anyone peeking in recognizing her. Same for him. He hated facing away from the door, but let Jason take the key position.

"Jason, this is Sheila." He relayed the information she'd told him.

"Nice to meet you, ma'am. Sorry this had to happen to you." Their order was called, and Jason retrieved it.

Mark sipped his drink. "Was this guy in an extra foul mood today?"

Sheila's hands shook, and she wrapped them around her cup. "We had our regular Monday morning meeting today. At the end of it, Carl was angry." She gulped down some coffee.

"What set him off?"

"I'm not sure. Before the meeting started, Carl was talking to this guy in the back corner. I'd never seen him before. Then, while the department heads were talking, the

114

stranger was mumbling and playing with something on a table beside the wall. He was distracting. I figured Carl would tell him to stop, but he just let him do it. At the end of the meeting, the president said some weird stuff and everybody filed out. Carl was angry and had a heated discussion with the president."

Mark wondered if the man had been mumbling the fake spell.

She shifted her cup back and forth. "Several people mentioned how much of a grouch he was after that."

Mark leaned forward. "What did the president say?"

She rubbed her forehead. "I'm not sure. Something about us doing whatever he, the vice president or Carl said to do."

Mark met Jason's disgusted gaze and turned back to Sheila. He had a feeling Carl had hoped he'd have full control over Sheila's response to him.

"The president finished with something like, 'Are we all in agreement?'" She shook her head. "You can imagine how people reacted to something like that."

Sheila was one of the people they'd tried the spell on. His anger rose for this woman who could have been subjected to the real spell—one he'd flippantly told Kristy to send. "What did Carl say just before he left your office?"

She bit her lip. "He threatened to hurt my daughter if I didn't..."

Mark covered her hand. "We aren't going to let that happen."

"How can you stop it? Before leaving, I emailed my resignation to human resources, but they'll give Carl my address, if he doesn't have it already."

He glanced at Jason, who gave a slight nod.

Mark shoved his cup aside and leaned forward. "This is what we're going to do. We'll pick up your daughter, then go to your house so you can pack for a couple of weeks. We'll have to stash you in a motel for a few hours while we take care of something first, then we'll take you with us to Rawlins."

Jason tapped the table. "I don't think she should stay at Mom and Dad's. With you and Kristy already there, she'd be extra incentive. I don't want them at my house with Shauna and the baby." He glanced at Sheila. "Sorry."

"Understood."

"I think I can call Adam and Trill to take them. With their abi...Anyway, nobody could get past them."

Mark frowned. "Who are Adam and Trill?"

"Do you remember the man who was kidnapped with Jamie?"

The guy who kind of went crazy who was the kidnapper's son? Yeah. Not mentioning that to Sheila. "Do you know where he lives?"

"He and his wife, and baby moved to Rawlins. Our wives are good friends. You'll like them."

"Um. Okay."

Jason took out his phone. "I'll give him a call." He dialed and held the phone to his ear. "Trill. It's Jason. How are you?"

A woman's voice responded, but the words were indistinct.

"They're good. Logan's only waking us once a night now.

The woman spoke again.

"She'll like that. I have a favor to ask. I'm helping a woman who was attacked by a co-worker. I'm hoping you can take in her and her daughter for a week or two while things settle down."

Jason listened to her. "Thanks so much. Sorry, it's going to be kind of late. Bye."

He put his phone away. "It's all set. They'll have a guest

room ready when you arrive."

"Thank you. Now it's time to get my daughter."

Mark hoped Carl didn't try to track down Sheila before they got her out of town.

***

Mark sat on the ground with his knees bent, a tree at his back, and a ski mask pulled over his face. A foot away, Jason echoed his position. Dusk would prevent the casual observer leaving the target building from seeing them at the edge of the woods. How many times had they sat just like this— ready for action, usually the worst kind? A bulletproof vests, handguns in shoulder holsters, knives at their ankles, and AR-15s in their hands, ready for anything.

Mark let out a long, slow breath. He was so tired of missions. Sure, he'd saved a lot of lives. Some individually, such as kidnapped politicians or wealthy people. Others, the more satisfying, were the times they took down a network of criminals. It protected a lot of people, most not realizing they'd been saved.

This time, though, beat all the others. He was here to protect Kristy. There'd been times when he or Jason had been arrested, mostly breaking and entering—in and out of the country—but Jack cut through the red tape and got them out. Sometimes, not so quickly. This time, there was no safety net. If they got arrested, it was all on them to get out.

Mark held a fist out. "Thanks, man, for doing this."

They fist bumped. "No thanks needed. This is important to both of us."

A man left the building and drove away in the second to last car.

Mark glanced at his watch. Already eight o'clock. It had been dark for a couple of hours already. He wanted to get back to Kristy. "Let's give it ten more minutes for that car to leave and go in either way."

"It's your show."

The minutes dragged on, and the car didn't leave. Mark stood. "Let's go."

They raced across the expanse of grass, making no sound. At the sidewalk, Mark slowed to a jog. He tried the door, not surprised it was locked. He'd already put his hand on his lock pick, and took it out. Forty-two seconds, and the lock clicked.

Jason whispered. "I could have done it in thirty."

"No, you couldn't."

Mark pocketed his pick, and yanked out his gun. He opened the door and stepped through. A god-awful tingle coursed through him. A protection spell, but something more—some kind of slimy stuff coated his skin. He rubbed at it, but his fingers only touched normal skin. The coating crawled over him like a colony of ants—slimy ants dragging cold blood.

He shivered again. "Hey, did you feel that? There's something extra in that protection spell."

"Feel what? Instead of reconnaissance, why don't we go talk to whoever is still here? We'll probably find out more than by poking around."

Mark glared at his friend. "Seriously?"

"Yeah."

Through the small holes in the mask, Jason's eyes appeared glazed, all the life sucked out of them. It had to be that slime stuff causing him to want to basically turn himself in.

Jason took a step. "Let's go."

"Stop. Let's think about this."

Jason paused, but his head stayed turned to the left, as if he knew exactly where to go.

Mark wouldn't be able to wrestle a determined Jason into leaving. He backed into the wall, thrust off from it, and raced toward Jason. He bent, struck Jason in the ribs with his shoulder and drove him back. Jason's foot caught on the threshold and he fell backwards with Mark half on top of him.

Mark jumped to his feet and toed Jason's legs aside so the door would close and studied his friend. He didn't know if whoever was in the building would know they'd come in, and when they didn't show, come and investigate.

The creepy-crawly sensation was gone, as if exiting the building had washed all the slime off. He hoped the same had happened to Jason. There was no way he'd take Jason by surprise again.

Jason sat up and rubbed his hands over his covered head, then repositioned the eye openings. "Did I just try to go talk to the head dude?"

"Yep. The protection spell slimed us."

"And you felt it?"

"Like a whole nest of ants crawling all over my skin. Come on, man. We have to get out of here."

Jason groaned as he struggled, and Mark grabbed his arm and yanked him up.

Mark broke into a jog and glanced over his shoulder. Jason had taken one step.

"Hurry!"

Jason picked up speed and caught up, so Mark increased his pace.

Jason grabbed the top of his head. "Every time my foot hits the ground, my head splits open."

They reached the SUV where they'd parked at a building with a second shift of workers, hiding the car among all the others. Mark held out his hand. "Give me the keys. I'll drive."

Jason tossed them, and Mark climbed into the driver's seat with Jason taking his place beside him. Mark snatched off the ski mask. Jason had tipped the seat back, and appeared asleep, except for the tension in his shoulders.

"Get your mask off. Do you have any pain reliever in here somewhere?"

Jason tugged off the mask, keeping his eyes closed. "Yeah, somewhere."

Mark pulled over and checked the console between the seats, found a bottle, and shook out three. "Here."

He grabbed a water bottle from the backseat and cracked it open, handing it to Jason. The man popped the pills in his mouth and chased them with half the water.

Mark got back on the road.

Jason dropped his bent arm over his eyes. "If this is how migraine sufferers feel, I sympathize with them. None of it affected you?"

"Not that way. I felt like I'd been slimed. Must be whatever makes me feel the protection spells also keeps out the extra. Thank God, or we'd both probably be dead. They must only set that up for when they're closed."

A short time later, Mark entered the motel parking lot, and turned off the car. "Do you think you can drive? It's probably best if I drive Sheila's car, just in case."

Jason tipped the seat up. "Headache's not gone, but it's tolerable now. Yeah, you drive her. We don't want her changing her mind and getting in trouble."

Mark strode to the motel room door and knocked. The peephole darkened and the chain and deadbolt slid.

Sheila opened the door and stepped back. "Rayne, honey, go use the bathroom. We're leaving in a minute."

Jason leaned into the doorway. "Give me the key, and I'll check you out."

She passed it over. This small, family-owned motel still

used real keys.

The dark-haired girl darted into the bathroom and closed the door. Mark grabbed the bag on the bed. The rest had remained in Sheila's trunk.

"If you don't mind, I'd prefer to drive. That way we can make sure we don't get separated." He hadn't been to Adam's house, but she didn't have to know that.

"That's fine. I don't like driving in the dark, anyway." She dropped the keys into his hand.

The bathroom door opened and the little girl came out. She gave him a big grin. "Hi, Mark." They'd hit it off when they first met. "Are you coming with us?"

"Yes. I'm going to drive you to our friends' house. They have a baby. Do you like babies?" If Rayne was like his nieces, she loved babies.

She clasped her hands. "Yes. A boy or girl?"

He wracked his brain. "A boy. Does it matter?"

Sheila chuckled. "Not at all, until they're about two, and then boys are just trouble."

"Let's get going." They got in the car and started the drive.

Mark and Jason had failed at finding out anything they could use, but at least they'd rescued Sheila. He just wanted to get back to Kristy.

He chatted mostly with Rayne until she fell asleep.

His phone rang. "Hey, Jason. What's up?"

"Pull over." His voice sounded tense.

A couple miles before, he'd seen a sign for a rest area. "About two miles up, there's a rest stop."

Jason huffed out a breath. "All right. Meet me there." He punched the phone to end the call.

"Your friend sounded like something's wrong," Sheila said.

He pinched his temples between his thumb and ring

finger. "Yeah, it has me worried."

Two minutes later, he followed the SUV into the rest stop, got out, and stood in the headlight glare between the two vehicles. "What's so important that this can't wait until we get back?"

Jason squeezed Mark's shoulder. Whatever it was, it wasn't good, and he didn't want to hear it. He tried to back up, but Jason squeezed harder, and stared into his eyes.

"Someone broke into the house, and knocked out Ward. They took Kristy."

With each word, the fear and pain mounted. He couldn't lose her. He'd ignored his gut reaction to leaving her, attributing it to leaving behind the woman he loved. On too many missions, his gut had saved his life, and this time, rejecting it could cost Kristy hers.

Mark shoved Jason against his car and pointed a finger at him. "You're the one who said she'd be safe with Ward, that he had experience."

"They broke the sliding glass door in the kitchen. He went to check it out, gun drawn. He said a force yanked the gun from his hand and cracked his head against the wall. When he regained consciousness, the door to the secret room was ajar." Jason touched Mark's arm, but he shook it off. "I'm sorry."

Mark's chest ached worse than when he'd gotten a bullet through a lung. The woman he loved was in the hands of madmen who would kill her if he didn't find her fast enough. "Give me your keys. I'm going back to Freeland Enterprises."

Jason grabbed Mark's shoulders and hung on. "You'd have to go in alone, and they'd take you down. She needs you alive to help her. Besides, they wouldn't take her to their business offices. It would be someplace private."

What Jason said made sense, but Mark wanted to tear

Carl to shreds. He wasn't the one to kidnap her, but he ordered it.

"Mark, we have experience rescuing kidnapped women. We can do this."

"Yeah. Like your sister? She was missing a month, and they didn't want her dead. The moment Kristy's usefulness is gone, they'll kill her."

In a lower voice, Jason said, "Then let's get this done. We'll drop off Sheila and her daughter, then go to my place to regroup."

Mark leaned, eyes closed, and palms planted on the warm hood of Sheila's car. He had to calm down and clear his head. No matter how much it hurt, how much he worried about Kristy, it would do her no good if he couldn't function. He drew in a long, slow breath and blew it out. Three more times and he was ready. Not good like normal mission good, but he could think now.

He straightened and stared at his friend. They'd been through a lot together, and Jason was the only man he trusted to help him get Kristy back.

Chapter 12

The light filtering through Kristy's eyelids caused enough pain to make her think of ice picks jabbing through them and into her brain. Opening them would be worse. She squeezed them tighter and buried her face in a pillow. That helped. A little. The scent was unfamiliar. She wasn't home, or at Shauna's, or the Ballard's. And that was bad.

Maybe someone watched her right now, and they'd seen her move. Knew she was awake. Since it didn't matter anymore, she wiggled her feet. Free of ties. She stretched her spine and flung her arms over her head. She might have a bruised rib but was otherwise good. Just her head wasn't fine.

All the years she'd gone to clubs and bars, she'd never been roofied. She didn't fool herself about why. She almost never said no when asked to leave with someone, and she never accepted a drink from anyone except the bartender. She did a mental assessment of her body. It didn't feel used, and she still had clothes on. The only issue was the spiky headache.

Despite the pain, it was time to check out her surroundings. Keeping her eyes closed, she scooted up with her back against the headboard, and drew her knees to her chest. She cracked her eyelids the tiniest bit. The pain didn't increase, so she opened them fully.

She sat on a cream-colored duvet covering a queen-size

bed. The medium blue throw rug beside the bed picked up the blue of ribbons in the flower vases on the wallpaper. The furniture in the room matched the oak flooring, and light streamed through the windows. It was an attractive prison.

At least, she wasn't in a dungeon or spider infested basement. That was a plus. No bars blocked the windows, but she wasn't likely on the first floor. A broken leg from jumping would hamper her escape.

She stared at the door, wondering if it was locked from the outside. She slipped a foot to the floor as a key slid into the lock. The doorknob twisted, and the door creaked open. A man stood in the doorway with a tray of food in his hands. Attractive, dark hair, tanned skin, and too many muscles for her to fight.

It all rushed back. This man, with the help of at least one other, had kidnapped her. She'd come out of the secret room, and Ward wasn't at the desk like the previous time. She should have gone back into hiding, but at the time, she'd thought he was either in the bathroom or finding a snack. She'd ventured into the foyer, and one of the men snatched her from behind. He'd yelled out that he had her.

She'd fought and kicked, but it did no good. Her only thought was that if they took her, she might never be free again. Then this man ran down the stairs and stabbed something into her neck. She touched the spot, finding it tender, and wondered if it was bruised. Just before she passed out, she'd seen head and shoulders of Ward on the kitchen floor. She hoped he hadn't died trying to save her.

As the man advanced with the tray, his gaze roved over her, making her shiver, in a bad way. She was glad she was conscious.

He advanced into the room and set the tray on the bed. "You can eat that or not. I don't care if you're hungry. And it's not drugged since we want you fully functional to correctly solve the cryptogram." He backed away. "You've got a half-hour before I come back. There're clothes in the dresser, and you can shower." The door closed and locked.

Mark. He must be frantic. She'd put him through so much pain when she left him, and now more than ever, she regretted those eighteen months they'd lost. Hope was hard to hold onto, but that's all she had.

Whatever was through that door, she'd show a brave face, delay the solution, and not let on they'd never get it, giving Mark a fighting chance to find her. This would be a difficult acting job, trying not to show her hands trembling, or let her face reveal her fear.

She and Mark had been searching for the bad guys' location for so long and had finally found that office building. She didn't know what they'd found, but it wasn't where she was now. Mark would have no clue how to find her.

Kristy sucked in a deep breath. She'd take the guy up on that shower but do it before eating. No way would he catch her naked. In the dresser, she found two flannel pajama shorts and tank tops. Not heartening since it indicated she'd be there a while. Beside them, a stack of sweats, an unopened package of panties, and socks filled the rest of the space. No bra. She'd have to wear hers again. Kristy wrinkled her nose as she grabbed a top and bottom. She didn't own sweats but given the way that guy had gawked at her, it was probably a good thing she'd be wearing baggy clothes. Usually, she enjoyed a man checking her out, but this man creeped her out. Not that she was interested anymore. She rushed through her shower and dressed.

Kristy popped the last piece of cold toast in her mouth as the door squeaked open. This was it. Time to find out what was on the other side. She stood on shaky legs and lifted her chin. She'd had a lot of practice leading boys and men to what she wanted.

These guys didn't know it yet, but this would be played her way.

***

Mark sat up with a groan. He'd hardly slept at all. So much for Jason saying, 'Let's sleep on this, and maybe we'll have better ideas in the morning.' He was just as tired as when he'd gone to bed, and no ideas had come to him.

He crushed the camisole clenched in his hand to his face. He'd found it the night before behind the bathroom door, still filled with Kristy's scent. It hadn't helped him sleep but had calmed him enough to relax his tense muscles.

He got up and tucked the camisole into his emergency bag from the car.

After a shower and clean clothes, he opened the bedroom door. He smiled at the faint baby cry down the hall. If Jason wasn't already downstairs, he would be soon.

In the kitchen, Mark set up the coffee maker, and before long the wake-me-up aroma filled the air. He poured a cup and took his first sip as footsteps clod down the stairs. Jason appeared more refreshed than Mark had in the bathroom mirror.

Jason took two mugs from the cupboard and filled both, then added cream to one. He sipped from the undoctored cup.

Dainty footsteps descended the stairs and Shauna stepped into the room. She laid Logan down in the bassinet and rushed across the room, throwing her arms around Mark's waist and dropping her head to his chest. "I'm so sorry. Jason told me this morning." A tear slid from her already red-rimmed eyes.

Mark's throat clogged. "We're getting her back."

She stepped away. "I know we will." She found her

coffee, took a sip, and sighed. "Should I make breakfast?"

He didn't think he could hold food in his stomach. "I'm good."

Jason kissed his wife's forehead. "Not right now, but you should eat."

Shauna grabbed a bowl from the cupboard and dumped a couple of oatmeal packets and water into it, then set it in the microwave. She leaned against the counter and crossed her arms. "How are we finding Kristy?"

Mark rubbed his temples. "I wish that spell you wrote would work for this."

Jason shook his head. "They'd have to try it again and be where Kristy is, which isn't going to happen."

Mark was desperate for anything. Nothing he thought of during the endless night would lead them to Kristy. "Don't you have some kind of spell to find people you know?"

"I wish it was that easy," Jason said.

The microwave dinged and the scent of apple-cinnamon oatmeal wafted the air when Shauna removed it. She poured on a splash of milk and stirred. "Yeah, if she had something one of us owned, we could do a find spell on that."

Mark's heart pounded at the first glimmer of hope. "What about a ring?"

Shauna frowned. "She doesn't have a ring, and the earrings she wears, she bought herself."

"I gave her an engagement ring."

Shauna's eyes widened. "You're engaged?" She dropped her spoon and threw herself at Mark. "I'm so happy for you both." She leaned back and frowned. "But she didn't tell me."

"She wanted to tell you in person and show you the ring." He rubbed his temples, doing nothing for the dull headache. "I'll be happy again, too, after I get her back."

Shauna bit her lip and narrowed her eyes. "I'm not sure

if the ring will work. I mean, it's worth a try, but you haven't really owned it before giving it to her."

He grinned, for once happy he'd almost proposed to her all that time ago. "It was in my possession for eighteen months before I gave it to her."

Shauna sucked in a breath and grabbed his hand. "You were going to propose to her before she broke up with you?"

He nodded and stared at his socked feet.

She rushed across the room. "Jason, you need to go get your mom's spell book and look up the find spell. Get the ingredients from the spell room and get back here ASAP."

For the first time in twelve hours, the band around Mark's heart eased. This spell would work. If it didn't work the first time, he'd make sure they did it again and again until they got it right and found Kristy.

A month ago, this whole scenario would be a fantasy, but he was immersed in the magic. It was what got Kristy into trouble, and it would help get her out of it, and back into his arms.

***

The same guy who left the food stopped in the doorway. "Pick up your tray and come with me."

Kristy did as he commanded and inwardly cringed at the way his gaze roved over her. She wore sweats for cripes sake. "Since I'm a guest here, mind telling me your name?"

He stared at her face for about five seconds. "Terrence."

"I'm Kristy, but you probably already know that." She took a step down the hall, not sure which direction they were supposed to go. "Okay, let's go, Terry."

"It's Terrence," he said through gritted teeth. "And we're going this way." He pointed in the opposite direction.

"My bad." Kristy turned one-eighty and sauntered down

the hall. If there was ever a time she wanted to make this man angry, she'd use the nickname but never when she was alone with him.

He caught up and stayed beside her. Yay for wide hallways and stairs. At least he wasn't behind, staring at her backside. Once at the bottom of the stairs, she noticed a tall, thin woman leaning against a doorframe. Her brown hair curled around her pretty face.

"Beth Ann, come take this tray," Terrence said.

The woman straightened and glared. "I'm not your servant."

"Just take it. I have to get her to Harrison's office."

Three first names, and she'd seen all their faces. Either they didn't think she'd be able to identify them later, or she wasn't leaving this house alive. Her breath hitched, but she steeled her nerves. She wouldn't get through this acting like a wimp.

The cup rattled against the plate as the tray shifted from Kristy's hands to Beth Ann's.

Terrence grabbed Kristy's upper arm. "Come on. This way."

He hauled her down a side hall and into an office with windows facing a manicured lawn and a tall, wrought iron fence. There was probably a gate across the driveway, too. Even if she could escape the house, she wouldn't make it over that fence.

Her gaze traveled around the room, intentionally ignoring the gray-haired man sitting at the desk. A monitor, keyboard, and mouse sat off-center, and a wire rack held several file folders. Maybe one was about her.

The best commercial grade carpet she'd ever had under her feet was two shades darker gray than the woodwork, which matched the ten feet of bookcases. Across from the desk a large oil painting with a scene of a sailing ship tossed by waves hung centered on the wall. It kind of described her life right now.

On a lark, she'd taken an art history course, thinking she'd have an easy pass. She'd worked hard for her A but enjoyed every minute. There'd been a unit on stolen art, and this painting seemed sort of familiar. She sure hoped it was a copy.

Figuring she'd taken enough time to show she had some control, she strolled to the chair in front of the desk and sat. She folded her hands in her lap, trying to appear prim—as much as possible in tacky attire.

"Miss Collins, what do you think of my office?" His blue-gray eyes twinkled. If she didn't know better, she'd think he was a loving grandfather.

She shrugged. "It would be a nice space to work in. Harrison, I presume."

The man's gaze flicked to Terrence, and he nodded. Terrence stepped into the hallway and closed the door.

"Miss Collins—"

"You can call me Kristy." Might as well make it seem like she would cooperate.

"Kristy, your solution to the second part of the cryptogram was incorrect."

She widened her eyes, hoping she showed surprise, and shrugged. "Sorry. I rarely make puzzle mistakes." It would be hard, but she could play oblivious. "You know, people don't usually get kidnapped because they mess up an online cryptogram."

The corner of his left eye twitched. "Ah, but this was no ordinary cryptogram, and you know it." One side of his mouth tipped up. He seemed to enjoy their conversation but didn't want to let on.

Kristy stretched her legs out and crossed her ankles. Stupid sweatpants. "I think all good puzzles are special in their own way."

"This one more than most." He leaned forward and laced his hands on the desk. "I want you to try again to solve it." He was trying to convey calm and control, but those rigid fingers gave away his tension. "You solved the first two parts perfectly. We tried to apply your solution to the rest, but it was incorrect."

She crossed her arms under her breasts and glanced down. The effect was totally lost in a sweatshirt. No matter. This man was too focused to get distracted anyway. "I don't usually revisit my errors. My motto is, forget it and move on." She was overjoyed that she'd been given the chance to revisit her worst error. An imaginary knife stabbed her heart. If a real one was in her future, at least she'd experienced true love.

Harrison shook his head. "Tsk tsk. Kristy, we learn by trying to fix our mistakes. I'll even give you some incentive. Six months of pay at the rate of the job you just lost. You can take time off while you search for the perfect employer."

She gripped the arms of the chair and shifted deeper into it. She hadn't expected him to investigate her life. Her best guess was that she wouldn't live to collect his payout. Or maybe he planned to use the newly cracked spell to turn her into whatever he wanted. Somehow, that seemed worse than dying.

She pasted on a grin. "That might make it worthwhile to fix my error."

He smiled, and she had the feeling that he was thinking 'gotcha.' "How long do you think it will take?"

This man may have investigated her, but that didn't tell him anything about the real Kristy.

"I'm not sure. Since I already messed this one up, it's obviously a difficult cryptogram." She shrugged. "It gets done when it gets done."

Harrison pursed his lips, and his eye twitched again. "Very well." He raised his voice. "Terrence."

The door opened, and Terrence swept her with a glance. "Sir?"

"Take Kristy to the office prepared for her."

"Yes, sir."

Kristy moved towards Terrence, and he gripped her arm. She'd yank away, except she had to show her cooperation.

Two doors down and on the opposite side of the hallway, he opened a door. She entered and crossed the room to the window.

"It won't do you any good. That overlooks an enclosed courtyard."

"I just wanted to see the view."

He pointed to a closed door. "That's the bathroom. Bottles of water beside the paper. Anything else you want?"

Scrawled across the top sheet of paper was the part of the cryptogram that Harrison didn't have the solution for.

"How about a computer?"

He chuckled. "You don't need one." He tapped his temple. "All you need is brain power."

"How about a sliced apple?"

His brows rose.

"You know. Cut an apple into eight pieces and remove the seeds. If you don't want to do that for me, you can bring me an apple and knife and I'll do it myself." They wouldn't trust her with a knife, but it couldn't hurt to ask.

He grinned and shook his head. "You're amazing. Most women would be curled up in a corner."

She wondered if he knew this from experience, but pushed the thought away. She needed to focus on the right attitude and staying safe. "That wouldn't do me any good." She propped her hand on her hip. "Since you're being so nice, can you get me some better clothes?"

He perused her from head to foot, making a long pause at her breasts. "What's wrong with those?"

"Seriously? Do you really think I'm a sweats kind of girl?"

"I can imagine you wearing short skirts and tight tank tops." His voice grew husky. "I can picture you even better out of them."

Oops. She'd pushed too far. A couple of years ago, this kind of flirting would get her the guy she wanted, but now, wrong guy, definitely the wrong situation. If she could help it, this man would never get his hands on her.

"Let's just start with the apple. Okay?" She sat in the chair, giving him her back.

"I'll see what I can do." He left, and the door locked behind him.

Kristy slumped in her chair and closed her eyes. That was intense. And she hadn't even done the hard part yet. She still had to delay solving the puzzle for a long, long time, and make them think she was working hard on it. Otherwise, there was no reason for them to keep her alive.

Chapter 13

Mark pounded away on the computer in Jason's office. Every search he'd done on Freeland Enterprises hit a wall—too many nested shell corporations. The bio on Freeland's website painted the CEO, Harrison Dalton, as squeaky clean. But it was in his building where they'd used Kristy's fake spell. A web search of information on the CEO turned up a couple of charity events and nothing more.

Maybe Mark's gut wrenching worry clouded his thinking. Usually, his thoughts clicked through exactly the path to take to dig out the information he needed. Now, there was nothing to help him find Kristy.

The front door opened and closed. "I'm back," Jason called out.

Mark sprinted from the office. Ready or not.

Jason set a bag on the kitchen table in front of Shauna. "I called Tony and asked him to get someone from Dad's maintenance crew to replace the door and sweep up the glass." Once he finished college, Jason's brother had joined their father in his business.

Mark squeezed the back of the chair as he leaned into it. They were one step closer to finding Kristy in this crazy magical world they'd been dropped into. "Did you find everything?"

"Yes." Jason plucked the pendulum from the bag. "And I

grabbed this from the desk." He fished out two bottles of herbs and a brown liquid. Next, he removed a small propane tank, holder, and beaker. Mark had seen Reese use those when he'd created his invisibility spell.

Mark peeked into the bag. "Where's the book?"

Jason grabbed his phone from his pocket. "I took a picture of the page. I didn't want to remove Mom's spell book from the house." He made eye contact with Mark. "You know that thing is over two hundred years old?"

"Let me see." Mark grabbed the phone and enlarged the crisp picture. He could read the ingredients easily enough— not that he was familiar with all of them. They *had* to get it right. Kristy's life might depend on it.

Jason fitted the small propane tank on the stand, then glanced at his wife. "Shauna, can you get your measuring spoons, and paper and pen? Mark, pull out your phone. I'll need to time this."

Mark opened his phone timer.

Shauna returned with the items. "Here." Jason passed the notepad and pen to Mark. "Write down the incantation. When I tell you, you'll have to say it three times."

"Me?"

"It's your lost item. Shauna, go get a tablet from my office and find a map."

She raced off to comply.

Mark wrote with care, not wanting to get any word wrong. He pushed the sheet to Jason. "Double-check it for me."

Jason bent over it. "Perfect." He read the recipe and measured dried, crushed leaves from the first bottle then dumped them into the beaker. He referred to the spell again and measured the second ingredient, then dumped it in. The third bottle was the liquid, and he measured three tablespoons, pouring all into the beaker. He swirled the flask.

"Time a minute."

Mark set the timer for one minute. Jason kept swirling. At the beep, he set the beaker on the stand.

Jason gripped Mark's shoulder and didn't speak until Mark met him eye-to-eye. "The rest is on you, buddy. From here to the end, you need to have that ring pictured in your head—in your hand, in its box, sliding it on Kristy's finger, on her finger. All of it, just keep running it through your mind."

Mark nod. "I can do that."

Jason slid Mark's phone to Shauna. "Honey, I want you to run the timer. Two minutes once I light the flame. Three minutes once I drop the pendulum in the beaker. One minute after I lift it out."

He turned back to Mark. "This is the toughest part. Once that one minute goes off, you have to grab the pendulum like this." It hit his palm, and he wrapped his fingers around it. "Don't let go until you've read that spell three times through."

"Ouch."

"Yeah, it burns like the dickens, but it shouldn't blister."

"Sounds like you speak from experience." Even if his palm blistered and all the skin fell off, it would be worth it if they found Kristy. If he had to do it a third or fourth time over the damaged skin, he'd keep going until he didn't have skin left.

"Long story for another time."

"I'll do this as many times as it takes for it to work."

Jason squeezed Mark's shoulder. "I know you will, man." He lit a match, twisted the knob on the propane tank and let them join in a whoosh. "Two minutes. Start imagining."

Mark imagined picking out the ring and the elation of presenting it to Kristy, opening the ring box over the months, wondering what had gone wrong. But he couldn't think about what was wrong, only what was right. He pictured the ring in his hand, cold at first, then warming, and how it looked as it slid onto Kristy's finger, and the perfect way it twinkled on her hand. He would see it in person again. He had to.

Beep. Beep. Beep.

Metal hit glass as the pendulum dropped into the liquid. "Three minutes."

Mark shuffled through his pictures again, trying to make them a part of him, trying to make that ring the most important thing in his life right now.

Beep. Beep. Beep. Glass clinked as the pendulum must have hit the side as Jason withdrew it. "One minute."

Mark rifled through his pictures again.

Beep. Beep. Beep. He held his left hand out, and Jason slapped the pendulum against it, and Mark closed his fingers. Whoa! Heated pain radiated into his palm. It reminded him of the time he'd grabbed a hot cast iron pan handle. He'd dropped the pan immediately, but now he tightened his grip around the pendulum. Since he had to read, too, he settled on one picture, the one where his hand had partially slid the ring onto Kristy's finger.

In a strong voice, he recited. "What I have lost, I must now find. Pendulum and map aligned, lead me to this object of mine." He repeated the words two more times.

He gazed at Jason.

Jason nodded. "Open your hand."

His fingers didn't want to straighten. It must be what arthritic people experienced in the morning. Millimeter by millimeter his fingers almost creaked open. Once it was wide enough, he grabbed the chain and swung the pendulum free. His palm and fingertips were an opaque white.

"You might want to run cold water on that."

Mark held his hand up and made his way to the kitchen

sink. He flipped on the cold water, then stuck his hand under the flow. Ah, relief. He hoped once was enough, but he wouldn't shy from doing it again. The stakes were too high.

After a minute, he patted his hand dry on a dish towel, then opened and closed his fingers. It hurt some, but worked fully.

He returned as Jason woke up the tablet with the map on screen.

Jason waved at the pendulum. "Pick it up. You're still the star."

Mark picked up the chain. "Hey, I didn't see a burn on your hand when you gave us the pendulum to find that building."

"It was a different spell that worked in reverse. It called the pendulum. Now you have the pendulum calling the ring."

Mark held the pendulum over the map, something he practiced a few times while Kristy slept. He'd never gotten a reaction. Although Jason hadn't said he needed to, he imagined the ring again. It couldn't hurt. The pendulum's swing slowed, but it never jerked to a spot. This had to work. They didn't have anything else to go on. He glanced at Jason.

His friend repositioned the map and expanded it. "Let's close in on the east coast more."

They were grasping at straws. From seeing how it had worked before, Mark knew this was a failure. He sighed. "Let's make it again."

"Are you sure you want to do this so soon?"

Anger tinged his voice. "That ring is out there on Kristy's finger." He waved at everything on the table. "For whatever reason, it didn't work, so we're going to figure out why not, and do it again. I'm not losing her." His voice cracked on the last.

Shauna picked up one of the bottles and stared at it. "Maybe it's not fresh enough. I'm sure Kathleen doesn't use these very often. Who knows how old they are."

"How do we get more? How long will it take?" It was one thing to repeat the spell, but if they had to place an online order for new ingredients, it might be too late.

Jason patted Mark's arm. "It's worth a try. Dad's store, Mystical Moment, should have them. They're common ingredients." He pocketed his phone and grabbed his keys. "I'll be quick."

Mark massaged his temples. It was crazy that Kristy's life hinged on fresh herbs.

***

Kristy ate an apple slice in two bites, as she stared at the page. Without the key, it would take her a while, but she knew the twists this particular cryptogram had, and that's what had taken her the longest last time. She scribbled the two letter words in a list and circled the ones that were the same. If memory served, these were all an A. She inserted the letter at every instance of the combination and crossed off the decoy letters. She'd been at this about an hour, and if someone checked on her, at least she had something to show for her time. She wasn't sure how long she'd allow before pretending to discover the other twist. Maybe not until tomorrow.

She wasn't usually this tense while working on puzzles. Normally they were exhilarating. A break might clear her mind. She strode to the center of the room, then stretched her arms above her head, and bent right and left. After a few minutes of various stretches, she performed deep knee bends. She never counted them, just stopped when it felt like enough. Her exercise routine had been sporadic over the past couple weeks, so she was sure this time she did fewer than usual. She patted her butt. At least she'd done enough reps to keep that in shape.

She finished with a few deep breaths, feeling more able to handle the juggling act. While still on the floor, the door opened.

Terrence frowned. "Why aren't you working on the cryptogram?"

Kristy stood and ran her hands down her sides. "I needed some activity. Getting my blood pumping helps me to think better."

His gaze traveled over her body.

She hoped this guy wouldn't end up being a problem. She wasn't used to having to fight for her virtue. "I'm ready to get back to the cryptogram." She sat in her chair and picked up a pencil.

The door closed, and she spun the chair to check that Terry was gone. She didn't want anyone sneaking up on her. He'd come in at the end of her workout, not surprised by what she was doing. He'd probably enjoyed watching her for a while on a monitor. She scanned the walls and ceiling, finding no camera lens. A closer inspection found a hidden camera in the wallpaper border near the ceiling. She found another that gave a different angle.

No surprise that they were watching her. She'd have to check the bedroom they'd put her in, not wanting to change where they could see her. And the bathrooms. An oily sensation slithered through her. She hoped no one had watched her shower and dress that morning. It should be her choice when she gave a show, and it wouldn't be for anyone here.

Back to the puzzle, Kristy worked out her timetable for her solution. It was kind of strange since she was used to going at it to get it done, and now she would pace herself. She drew up the possible solutions for the two letter words.

The door opened and she twisted around. "Oh, nice.

Lunch. I could use the energy. Thanks."

Terrence set a tray beside her. His gaze roved over her work papers. "You haven't accomplished much."

She lifted a sheet. "Here, you want to give it a try?"

He raised his hands. "Not me. We all gave it a shot and got nowhere."

Kristy shook the paper. "Then don't complain about my speed. The word 'a' was disguised as two letters. And you can bet that there are other twists in here. I want to finish this, collect my money, and get out of here. So, back. Off."

He stepped away. "All right. All right." The door locked behind him. She hoped he'd tell Harrison about the twist since that should buy her time.

Kristy ate the chicken salad on wheat bread, then attacked the brownie. At least they were feeding her well. Quite often at her job, if she wasn't going out for lunch, she'd work on a puzzle while she ate, but not here. She could burn up time by enjoying her meal and not thinking about the cryptogram.

By the end of the afternoon, she had pretended to solve two of the repeated two letter words.

As dusk approached, the door opened. She expected to either receive a dinner tray or be taken to her bedroom for dinner.

Terrence led her in a different direction. "Harrison would like you to join him for dinner."

"As long as he doesn't mind I'm not dressed for dinner." She didn't care that she wore sweats for this man, but she would have preferred eating alone in the room they'd assigned her.

Terrence waggled his eyebrows. "I wouldn't mind having dinner with you when you're not dressed."

"You seriously think I'd go along with that?"

His hand tightened on her arm. "I can be persuasive."

She didn't like the sound of that, and hoped Mark rescued her before Terrence followed through on whatever he had in mind.

They stopped in a doorway of a dining room. Harrison sat at the head of a long table covered in a burgundy tablecloth. One place setting sat to the right of his. He lifted a hand. "Kristy, come join me. Thank you, Terrence. Return in an hour."

Kristy crossed the oak flooring and took the indicated seat. "Good evening, Harrison." Her heart pounded at the thought he'd question her on her progress with the cryptogram. It was easier, she was sure, to lie to Terrence about the work than for this man to believe her. She hoped he wasn't angry that she hadn't solved the puzzle yet. She had a feeling bad things happened when he was angry.

He poured white wine into two fluted glasses as a woman entered, carrying a large tray. Her dark, upswept hair showed threads of white, and her gray dress was so drab it couldn't be anything but a uniform. She removed covers from plates and set them in front of Harrison and her. She added a basket with rolls between them and poured water from a pitcher on the table into their goblets.

"Anything else, sir?"

"That will be all. Thank you, Marta."

The woman nodded and left the way she'd come.

The aroma of chicken and mashed potatoes covered in a mushroom gravy, and long green beans with slivered almonds made her stomach growl. She didn't know etiquette in this situation, but she'd wait for Harrison to start eating. He cut and buttered a roll, so she did the same, setting it on the small plate beside her silverware.

"Eat, my dear. Marta is a wonderful chef."

Kristy dug in. The chicken was among the best she'd had at upscale restaurants.

Harrison sipped his wine. "Terrence tells me that the cryptogram is proving difficult."

"It's not your average puzzle." In so many ways. "It'll just take longer to solve."

"But you can do it?" The corner of his left eye twitched, and Kristy wondered what hidden emotion it was giving away.

"Of course." Because, if she said she couldn't do it, she'd be dead. Delay. Delay. Delay.

He tipped his glass to her. "You seem very confident."

"I started working puzzles when I was five. More and more difficult ones since then." She didn't want to tell this guy about herself. She had to make them think she was all in, even though this relationship started with her kidnapping, and she wouldn't be allowed to leave.

After that, he kept the conversation light and inconsequential. Although she was pretty sure she hadn't shown fear, Kristy was exhausted by covering it with a bubbly attitude.

With the hour up, Terrence stepped into the room, and she didn't think she ever would have been happy to see him, but hopefully, it meant she'd go back to the bedroom and have the night to herself.

Harrison tipped his head up. "Ah. Your escort has arrived. Thank you for a lovely dinner, Kristy."

She stood. "It was an interesting evening. I'll...ah...see you tomorrow."

She strode past Terrence, but he grabbed her arm, stopping her. "It's this way."

"Oh, I'm all turned around." She let him lead. "Marta is a terrific cook."

"Yeah, her meals are a nice perk when I work here."

She tried to keep track of where they were going. "You don't always work here?"

"No. Only when we have...guests."

That was a scary thought. He was referring to guests like her who were actually prisoners. She wondered what happened to the others.

She took a step after he stopped, and he yanked her back. "Here's your room."

Terrence didn't release her when they entered. She tugged, but he didn't get the hint. He grabbed her other arm and tugged her body up to his. "There's a long evening ahead. Maybe we should get sweaty together."

Kristy glared. "It might be nice to get some cardio in. Alone."

"After what I did for you?"

She raised her eyebrows. "What did you do for me?" Besides kidnap her, but she wouldn't mention that.

He pointed at the bed. "I bought you new clothes. I think you'll appreciate them more than the sweats. I know I will."

Sure enough, a couple of shirts similar to her own, a pair of pants, and a skirt lay across the bed.

She shoved away from him. "I'm not a hooker. I don't exchange sex for gifts. And you probably put those on an expense account."

He chuckled. "You're a smart one." He opened a door on a wall cabinet, revealing a screen. "Something else you can do this evening is watch television." He tapped a stack of books beside it. "Or read."

He wrapped a hand around the back of her neck, but she didn't fight him. Yet. "Maybe tomorrow you'll be more amenable. Sweet dreams, Kristy."

He probably didn't force the issue since Harrison still needed her to solve the cryptogram, and he might not survive if he hampered her work on it.

After the door locked, she stared at her beautiful ring and spun it around and around. Mark's state of mind bothered her. She was more worried about how her death would affect him than about actually dying.

She sunk to the bed, and took a long, relaxing breath. She sure hoped she'd played this right to buy her the most time. More than twenty-four hours had passed, and she wasn't sure how Mark would find her. Maybe tomorrow she'd have to keep an eye out for a way to get out of the house. And away from Terence before he put actions to his words.

Chapter 14

Mark's stomach churned as Shauna made ham and cheese sandwiches while he sat at the kitchen bar. Her jerky movements proved she was as upset as him over Kristy's kidnapping. He didn't know if he could stomach eating right now, but years of being in the field told him to eat while he had the chance.

The front door opened then closed. He tensed. If Jason hadn't found all the ingredients, they could try mixing old and new with the hope that whichever one was bad had been replaced.

Jason strode into the room and set his bag on the table. "I got it all. We had to search the back room for one of them." He gave his wife a peck on the cheek.

The baby cried from his bassinet. Jason nudged Shauna. "You two start eating. I'll go change Logan."

Shauna set a plate of sandwiches in the center of the table and three smaller plates at their seats. She sat in her usual place and nibbled a sandwich. "I would have skipped lunch altogether except I need to feed Logan."

Mark stood from the bar, but was too wired to sit at the table. He'd rather skip food and repeat the spell. The delay in finding Kristy shredded his control. He selected a sandwich and took a huge bite that might as well have tasted like sawdust. He washed it down with water and finished the sandwich. He couldn't enjoy anything until Kristy was safe. He ran his hands through his hair, tugging, needing to feel something other than the fear squeezing his chest.

Jason returned with a quiet Logan, and Mark held out his hands. "I'll take him." A much needed distraction. The other two ate while he paced and traded stares with Logan. The warm bundle calmed him, and the pain he'd had in his gut since learning of Kristy's kidnapping eased. He freed one of the baby's hands and kissed the soft skin, and wondered how holding a baby could lessen his worry.

In the back of his mind, he'd dreamed that someday he'd marry and have a family. His parents' marriage was solid, and his brother and sister were among his best friends, not that they'd always seen eye-to-eye. That's what he wanted with Kristy. If he lost her, he didn't think there could ever be another woman who could give him that life.

Shauna stood beside him. He hadn't noticed her leave her chair. "I'll take him now. I can still man the timer while I feed him."

Jason spilled the contents of his sack on the table. "You ready to try this again?"

Mark rubbed the whitened skin on his palm. "Yes. I'm ready to burn again if it finds Kristy."

Jason grabbed the rinsed out beaker from beside the sink, and double checking the spell on his phone, measured the ingredients. The herbs were greener than the previous ones, so maybe it would work this time.

Mark recalled images of the ring, and slid the paper with the spell in front of him as the timer counted down Kristy's destiny. He could recite the words without reading it, but he wasn't chancing messing up. He rubbed the burn from earlier—warm, but didn't hurt. He wouldn't let it stop him from doing anything for his woman.

The countdown ended, and Jason swung the pendulum

toward him. "Here you go."

Mark grabbed it with his right hand. If anything, it burned worse than earlier, but he didn't release it. He concentrated on the image of the engagement ring on Kristy's finger and recited the spell three times with careful precision. He didn't think it was possible, but the pendulum heated even more for a few seconds, but he maintained his tight grip.

"I think it worked." He uncurled his fingers and removed the pendulum. He sported a white burn patch that matched the other hand. After cooling his hand in running water, he grabbed the pendulum's chain. "Let's give it a try."

Jason called up the map on the tablet and slid it toward Mark. He held the weight over the United States. Its swing slowed then tugged eastward. "Yes!"

Mark expanded those states and worked his way to a city, then expanded to a neighborhood. Finally, the pendulum hovered over one building. "It's a house. More like a mansion."

He set the weight down, the relief making him light-headed. They had Kristy's location. "We need to go." He jumped up.

Jason grabbed his arm. "No. First, we're doing research. Who owns the house? What's he do? Maybe even find associates. Come on, man, you're the one who's usually on top of this."

Mark rubbed his temples. Jason was right. Going in blind, they could hit all kinds of unexpected obstacles and even fail. Research would give them an edge to recover Kristy alive. The hardest part was delaying going after her.

"Okay. Jason, why don't you find out about the owner of that house? I'll see if I can get some floor plans."

Mark had retrieved floor plans before—most recently when he assisted Jason in rescuing Jamie. She'd been hidden in the basement of an office building. He hoped he'd have the same success with Kristy being held inside a house.

He opened his laptop, and finessed his way into the town building department records. The house had been built in 1892. They probably didn't have records of plans back then, and even if they did, they wouldn't be online. He poked around more in case something useful showed up. There. A major remodel had been done ten years before. Four bedrooms had been divided in half and made into two bathrooms each, attached to the bedrooms on either side of them.

Kristy would likely be in one of those, at least at night. Would they take her to a different room to work on the cryptogram or leave her in a bedroom? A nighttime rescue might be best to increase the chances of finding her quickly. Mark hoped they weren't keeping her in the basement—for her sake as well as for their search. A first floor plan was included so they would be able to locate the stairs, and hopefully, avoid occupied areas.

"I've got floor plans. You have anything, Jason?"

"The owner is Harrison Dalton. There's the connection to Freeland Enterprises."

"Good. Anything else on Dalton?"

Jason grimaced. "I can't find anything illegal on him. There are instances where he skirted the law, but never crossed it. Right now, he's lobbying politicians in his state to reregister a huge tract of land Freeland owns from conservation to residential. He wants to build a two-hundred unit condominium complex."

Mark whistled. "That might make them need a strong influence on lawmakers. How long have they been working on it?"

"Two years. Maybe they got tired of hitting a wall."

Mark leaned his elbows on his thighs. "Okay. We have a possible why. Only problem is, law enforcement wouldn't believe how Freeland plans on getting the change put through." Jason opened his mouth, but Mark held up a hand. "And we don't want them to know. It's been two years. They must have some nefarious ways they've tried that can be pinned on them."

"Now that we've narrowed it down, I'll get on that." Jason spun back to his computer.

If they wanted to end Dalton's interest in Kristy, they'd have to get him arrested. The guy who'd kidnapped Jason's sister had also murdered a few men. The police were all too willing to step in and arrest the people involved.

Likely, Dalton also had murders under his belt, but they had no way to find out. He hoped kidnapping charges would hold—but how to explain to the police the reason Dalton had kidnapped Kristy.

Mark got up and paced. He needed to get down there ASAP. Maybe he couldn't do anything right away, but at least he'd have eyes on the house. "I'm calling Trey and Zack." He'd worked with them for years, and had trusted his life to them many times.

Jason glanced up. "Backup? It's probably a good idea."

"I wasn't thinking backup. I thought they could research any deaths connected to Harrison Dalton. Something that most people would have overlooked but could be related directly to him. Maybe benefited him. All right. Let's go. Now."

Jason rounded the desk, leaned back against it, and crossed his arms. "No. We have to do daytime reconnaissance. If we leave now, it'll be dark when we get there, so we won't accomplish anything. We'll gather more information and leave tomorrow.

Mark ground his teeth, but admitted that's what he would have said—if he gave himself a chance to think with his head and not his heart. By the time they attempted a rescue—not attempted, but rescued—Kristy would have been held for more than fifty hours. More time for something to happen to her.

***

Kristy leaned against the window molding, enjoying the view of sweeping lawns and scattered flowerbeds. She'd been relieved that Harrison hadn't invited her to dinner again. And even more so when Terrence hadn't insisted on staying while she ate. She'd gotten to savor Marta's marvelous manicotti alone.

It was unfortunate this window faced east. Morning sunlight brightened the room way too early, and like now, she didn't get to see the sunset. A pale reflected orange bathed the sky, making her think the real sunset was impressive. She'd love to see it with Mark right now, snuggled in his arms, watching the flaming sun sink out of sight.

She crossed her arms on the window frame between the locks, and rested her chin on her forearm. If only this was the first floor. She could take her chances trying to get over the fence, but not if she broke her leg jumping from the second floor window.

She'd been strong all day, setting just the right pace as she worked the puzzle, deflecting Terry's advances, and taking time, but not too much time with her meals and exercises.

One more day. She couldn't see any way to delay longer. By the end of the day tomorrow, she'd have to give them the solution. Or a solution. Dare she give them the wrong one again? That might gain her a night if she gave it to them just before dinner. Once they realized it was wrong, would they try to force her to correct it? Or kill her out of anger?

She rubbed her thumb on her ring. Mark. It would be

nearly impossible to find her. Time was running out.

She sighed. Maybe the book she'd started the night before would distract her, and eventually tire her enough to sleep. She grabbed pajamas and changed in the bathroom. In her search of the room, there'd been no cameras, but Terrence might come in while she was half dressed.

Kristy came out, plumped pillows against the headboard, and pulled the covers up under her arms. She grabbed the book from the nightstand, and opened it to the folded-down page—not something she normally did to mark the place she left off, but, hey, the book belonged to the bad guys.

Sometime later, after it was dark out, Terrence burst into the room. "Get up. We're leaving." He held a gun, pointed at the floor.

"What? Why?" Her heart pounded. She climbed out of bed and stood beside it, hoping he didn't decide to point the gun at her.

"I don't have time for this. Get your shoes on."

"But I'm in pajamas!" She didn't like this, but what was there to like about a kidnapping? Something had Terry in a blather.

He gritted his teeth. "Get your shoes on now, or you're leaving without them."

She scrambled into her shoes, then he grabbed her arm, and tugged her into the hallway. He dragged her to the left instead of the right. She yanked, but he didn't release her, only squeezing harder.

"What are we doing?" she asked.

"We need to get out of here. Now, stop talking."

Something strange was going on. "Does Harrison know we're leaving?"

"Not yet. Keep your mouth shut."

Chances were they weren't running from someone worse than Harrison. Maybe Terrence was trying to keep her out of the hands of rescuers. And he'd succeed if she didn't do something. She dragged in a huge lungful of air and screamed as loud as she could.

Terrence backhanded her. "I said shut up."

She fell against the wall. That hurt more than she expected. Her cheek stung and she covered it. Her cold hand calmed the pain. With her hope of rescue fading, she had to try again. She inhaled to scream, but his fist came at her face, and pain smacked into her jaw. Light exploded behind her eyes, then went dark.

***

Mark prowled the edges of Harrison Dalton's property. He should have studied satellite views of the house, but he'd let his emotions muddle his thinking. The six-foot wrought iron fence was a surprise—a problem they needed to solve.

Jason studied the top of the fence. "Except for the spikes, we could scale it."

"Yeah, I don't want to be stuck on top with a couple of spikes in my gut." Mark rubbed his temples. Stymied by a fence from getting to Kristy. But keeping people out was exactly the purpose for the fence. "How about a ladder?"

"We could get over, but then we'd be stuck on the other side with no way back."

Mark stared at the top of the fence. "We need two ladders. One for each side. I can climb up this side, and you can hand me the second ladder to put on the other side."

"That could work," Jason said. "We'd have to drop the one on the outside and lay the inside one flat until we get back to it." No sense having someone see the ladders and raise an alarm.

"Do the A-frame ones unfold all the way open?"

Jason shrugged. "I don't know. Dad's got an extension

ladder."

Mark rubbed his temples. "I hate to get extension ladders because they're noisy. If those A-frames work right, we'll get those."

Mark broke into a jog. "Let's go find a home improvement center."

Two hours later, they parked a half mile up the road on a little track leading into the woods. They each hauled a twelve-foot aluminum multi-position ladder, folded in half. That's what they were actually called. They retraced the path they'd found earlier heading toward the Dalton property. The trail cut parallel to the fence about fifty yards away.

They'd discussed the merits of placement to and from the store, and decided on a side, halfway down the length of the mansion. Just inside the tree line, they opened the ladders to their full height and set them on the ground.

Dusk had started to fall, coloring the sky in shades of pink. "Let's make a last perimeter run before it gets too dark. I want to make sure they don't let dogs out for the night or have a guard patrol."

They stayed in the shadow of trees. Every so often, they trained their binoculars on the lighted windows. Halfway across the back, Mark spotted her. "Kristy," he whispered. She leaned against the window, her sad expression tearing at his heart, but lifting it as well. He'd been afraid to hope that they'd find her here. What had she been through?

Jason's hand dropped onto his shoulder. "That's a lucky break. Let's check your floor plans. Count the doors for that room. I thought we'd have to try them all."

There was barely enough light to see the diagram Mark extracted from his thigh. They counted windows on the building and floor plan, and pinpointed Kristy's room, then traced the route.

Mark tucked the plan away. "Let's finish the perimeter."

At the road, they retraced their steps to the ladders. He sat, and leaned against a tree. They'd have to wait for full darkness before crossing the lawn.

The light remained on in Kristy's room. The end of the ladder caught Mark's attention. "Hey, what if we lean one of the ladders against the building under Kristy's window? We wouldn't have to pass all kinds of security cameras or guards."

"Do you think it'll reach?"

"Close enough that I could guide her down to it."

Jason checked his watch. "Ten minutes until it's full dark."

Time crept by, and Mark's skin crawled. After eight minutes he stood. "Let's go."

He grabbed one ladder and leaned it against the fence, then climbed to the top. Jason handed him the second ladder, and he lifted it over the fence and lowered it to the ground, leaning it against the fence. He hopped over the tops and scrambled to the ground.

At the top, Jason lifted the outer ladder over the fence and handed it to Mark, who laid it on the ground. Jason climbed down the ladder, and tipped it down. Each man picked up an end and they raced across the lawn. They rested it against the wall two feet under the window, then Jason drew his gun, making a sweep of the yard.

Mark climbed the ladder and peeked into the window. "No!"

Kristy tugged and dragged her feet as a man with a gun yanked her out the door. If they'd gone when he'd thought about using the ladder at the window, they could have rescued her.

Without taking his gaze off the open door, he whispered down to Jason. "An armed man just took Kristy."

Chapter 15

Mark smashed his elbow through the window, glad he was wearing a leather jacket, then used his gun to clear glass clinging to the frame. He wrapped a hand around the inside windowsill and scrambled through. A slight zing of a protection spell rippled through him. At least it wasn't the slimy one they'd encountered at the office building, so Jason wouldn't have a problem with it.

He hadn't expected to have to rescue her from a second kidnapping, but he'd do whatever it took to get her back.

He leaned through the window. Jason was halfway up the ladder. "They went left." Kristy's scream drove his heart into his throat as he raced out of the room. As he rounded the corner, halfway down the hall a door closed. He dashed to the door, relieved it wasn't locked as he forced it open. Stairs. He paused a moment. Footsteps and huffing from below. He rushed down, flying around a landing as the door at the bottom closed.

With a crash, Jason burst through the door at the top. "I've got your six."

Mark swung the door open and panned the hallway. A dozen feet away a man fled with Kristy flung over his shoulder, her arms dangling.

Mark planted his feet and raised his gun, Jason's reassuring running steps behind him. "Stop or I'll shoot."

The man never paused. Mark fired, and the man's knee buckled. He tumbled onto Kristy's legs, and her upper body flung back, her head striking the carpeted floor. Mark sprinted to the pair and yanked the gun from the man's hand, then shoved him off Kristy.

Jason hustled up and zip-tied the man's hands behind his back, took out his phone and called the police.

The man roared. "You won't get away with this. Harrison won't let you."

Mark sat against the wall with Kristy's unconscious body in his lap. A bruise marred her cheek. He buried his face in her neck.

Jason's voice registered. "Yes. Kidnapping. You'll have to get through a locked gate. Oh, and send an ambulance. A man's been shot."

Mark cradled Kristy and skimmed a finger down her good cheek. "Kristy, honey. You're safe now." He kissed her, hoping she'd wake up like Snow White.

Her arm flew up and knocked the side of his head.

He held her closer. "It's okay. You're safe."

Her eyes shot open. "I thought you were Terrence." She wrapped her arms around his neck. "I knew you'd find me."

With her in his arms, it felt like he'd gotten his life back. It almost hadn't happened. If they'd been any later, she would have been gone again. He touched her bruise. "Other than this, did they hurt you?"

"No. They treated me okay. They wanted to make sure I continued solving the cryptogram."

Sirens in the distance drew closer. Jason nudged the man on the floor, who groaned. "I'm going out to talk to the police. I don't want anyone sending them away. You okay here?"

Mark trained his gun on the man, who squirmed and glared. "We're good." Low on the floor like they were, he'd be able to protect Kristy from anyone entering the hall.

Jason jogged down the corridor.

The man glared at the two of them. Kristy pointed at him. "He's Terrence. If you want to make him angry, you can call him Terry."

"Baby, I think he's already angry that I shot him."

"He's one of the men who took me from the Ballards'."

Any guilt Mark had over shooting this man, melted away. If he didn't have to displace Kristy to do it, he'd kick him.

A few minutes later, two paramedics rolled a stretcher down the hallway. One squatted beside Terrence.

"Don't cut him free," Mark said. "He kidnapped this woman, and when he saw we were here to rescue her, he tried to take off with her." He patted Kristy's arm. "Let's get off the floor. Jason should be back soon."

After standing, he leaned against the wall with Kristy against him. His world was finally right again. "I was so worried about you." He kissed her temple.

Usually, his responsibility on a mission was coordinating police and the team, but he couldn't let Kristy out of his sight.

He sure hoped Harrison Dalton was at home, so he could be rounded up with whoever else was present. The man would get out on bail and might still be a threat if he thought Kristy could solve the puzzle. He'd try to use it on the right people and get the charges against him dropped.

Jason appeared at the end of the hall with two police officers in tow.

Kristy grabbed Mark's shirt. "Shauna! Can I use your phone to call her?"

He fished it from his pocket. "Sure, honey. She probably can't sleep until she hears if we rescued you."

The paramedics lifted Terrence onto the stretcher.

159

Mark took a few steps closer, never letting Kristy go as he spoke to the police officer. "He was one of the men who kidnapped Kristy from the house on the orders of Harrison Dalton."

One officer cut the zip-tie off and put handcuffs on Terrence. "I'm accompanying you to the hospital." He started reciting the Miranda rights.

The other officer stepped closer to them as Kristy handed Mark's phone back. "I know it's late, but you'll have to come to the station to make a statement."

"Can I change into day clothes first? I really don't want to go to the police station in pajamas."

The officer glanced at his partner, who shrugged. "All right. I'll come with you in case we haven't rounded everyone up yet."

Mark and Kristy walked hand in hand up the stairs and to the room she'd occupied, and the officer waited outside for them.

She grabbed clothes that he thought were her own, and she tugged a new pair of panties from a bag in the dresser drawer. She strode to the bathroom but didn't close the door. "Oh, yuck."

Mark should have checked that the bathroom was empty before allowing her to go in. He rushed to the doorway and stopped. "What's wrong?"

A bra dangled from her hand. "I washed my bra when I changed to pajamas, figuring it would be dry by morning. And since it's not morning..." She shook her head. "I can't put this on."

He grinned. "I don't mind."

"Of course you don't. Here." She tossed it at him. "I'm not leaving it with them."

He stuffed the damp clothing into his jacket pocket and leaned his shoulder against the door frame. After the scare of her kidnapping, he needed his Kristy fix, but the closest he'd come at the moment was to watch her change. His arms ached to hold her, his lips itched to touch hers, and do so much more.

She left the pajamas on the floor and stepped in front of him.

He hugged her and stared into her eyes. "I love you. I've been going crazy the past couple of days. Let's get out of here so I can do what I really want to do with you."

They met up with Jason and the police in front of the house. The same officer who'd accompanied them earlier strode up to them. "You'll need to come to the station to give statements."

Kristy crowded into Mark, probably thinking about being separated at the station, like he was.

"We'll follow one of your cars there," Jason said.

"We'd prefer if Miss Collins rode with us."

No way in hell was Mark letting her out of his sight until he absolutely had to. The officer probably figured they'd get their stories straight on the way over, which was his plan.

Mark lifted his chin. "No. She's suffered enough trauma and separation."

The officer shrugged. "Fine. You can both ride in the back of my car."

Mark swung around and called out. "Hey, Jason." His friend lifted his head, and Mark gestured to the officer standing beside him. "This officer is taking us to the station."

"All right. See you there."

The officer led them to a cruiser and opened the back door. "Hold on. Give me your gun."

"I'm not a suspect. There's no reason for me to give up my gun."

"And I'm not going to let someone with a gun sit at my back."

Mark sighed. "Fine." He raised his voice. "Jason?"

His friend walked up to them. "What's up?"

"He doesn't want me behind him with my gun." He slowly opened his jacket and lifted the gun out between thumb and forefinger. "Can you lock it in your truck?"

Jason's gaze flicked to the policeman before accepting the gun. "Sure. I'll see you there."

Mark's neck prickled as he gestured for Kristy to get into the car. He cast a quick glance around, and didn't see anything to cause him alarm. Something bothered him, but he wasn't sure what yet. He slipped in beside her, and she grabbed his hand.

The officer shut the door and took the driver's seat. His partner was getting into the ambulance with Terrence.

On the way to the building where Kristy was held, Mark and Jason had exited the interstate and driven away from the city center. The home improvement store had been between the house and downtown, but that should be where the police station was, and that wasn't the direction they headed.

"Where are we going?"

The officer tipped his head and met Mark's gaze in the mirror. "I'm taking the two of you in for questioning."

Kristy glanced at him, a furrow between her brows and tipped her mouth to his ear. "Is something wrong?"

He buried his face in her neck. "Something doesn't feel right." He'd been so thrilled to get Kristy back that he hadn't paid attention. It was a stupid, amateur's mistake.

She stiffened, and he wished he hadn't said anything, but she should be prepared.

They rode longer than it should have taken to get to the nearest police station. Now, the landscape was familiar. No way. He had a feeling they were being taken to Freeland Enterprises, with the slimy control spell protecting it. What would it do to Kristy?

They turned into the parking lot for Freeland Enterprises. Kristy poked his chest, and mouthed, "Freeland?"

He hadn't had a chance to tell Kristy the results of their visit after she was kidnapped.

Mark twisted as he removed his phone from his pocket, shielding his movement from the officer. He sent a quick text to Jason. *Freeland. Help.* Not that Jason could enter the building, but he could be there to pick them up after Mark figured out how to get out of this. He'd probably call the cops. They couldn't all be on Freeland's payroll.

The cruiser parked in the space closest to the door, and the officer pulled out his gun before opening Mark's door. He stepped back. "No fast moves or you're dead. Remember, we don't need you. We only need her."

Mark stepped from the car and pulled Kristy up behind him. She tried to step in front of him, but he didn't let her. She probably had some brave idea that she could be his shield. Wasn't happening.

The officer followed them to the door. "Open it and go inside."

Mark opened the door and wrapped one arm around the front of Kristy's shoulders and the other around her waist. He hoped since she'd felt the protection spell around the secret room when he touched her, holding her would protect her from the slimy spell.

Together, they stepped across the threshold, and her shoulders relaxed. No! A quick check of her eyes found them glazed. He dropped his arms from around her, and stared into the distance, pretending it affected him. He tried to ignore the creeping, slimy ants all over him.

The officer holstered his gun. He must have thought he was safe now. How many other people had this officer marched into this building? Jason had told Mark how a spelled medallion had affected him, and Mark wondered if this man wore a medallion to protect him from the spell or if he'd been excluded another way.

The man turned away. "This way." Kristy kept pace behind him.

Mark could jump the man and get them out of there, but maybe he should let it play out a little longer. Maybe get some important information to finish this for good. But if they ended up in a room with several men, he might not be able to fight his way out and take a hypnotized Kristy with him.

Mark took two quick, silent steps and wrapped an arm around the officer's neck. He unclipped the man's gun and removed it. Kristy bypassed them and kept walking. His heart leaped to his throat. He couldn't let her get to the programmed destination.

He hit the officer on the head with the gun grip, zip-tied his wrists and ankles, then dragged him out of sight into the nearest room. He checked the guy's neck for a necklace and found one. He yanked it over the man's head, hoping this was the protection Kristy needed.

Mark raced after Kristy. He caught up with her as she approached a turn in the hallway. He hauled her back out of sight and dropped the necklace over her head. Her eyes closed for a few seconds, and when they opened, they were clear. "Mark?"

He gave her a quick hug. "Welcome back. Let's get out of here."

Carl Gretsky came around the corner and trained a gun on them. "I don't think so. I told Harrison he should have brought her here. I'm sure with my encouragement she would have solved the cryptogram already."

Mark didn't want to know what Carl would have used for encouragement, but it wouldn't have been good for Kristy. And probably would be worse now.

Carl pointed the gun at Kristy. "Drop the gun."

Since the man wanted Kristy to solve the puzzle, he wasn't likely to kill her, but Mark couldn't take the chance that Carl wouldn't mind giving her some other injury. Mark dropped the gun and kicked it away.

Carl waved the gun muzzle. "Get moving. I'll tell you where to turn."

Mark settled his arm around Kristy's waist and walked beside her. It wasn't often someone held a gun at his back, and he especially didn't like it with Kristy at his side. If Carl shot him, what would he do to Kristy once she solved their puzzle? Sheila Michaels came to mind. No matter what, he couldn't give Carl the chance to touch Kristy.

"Turn left into that conference room."

A long wooden table with about twenty wheeled chairs around it sat in the middle of the room. Several more chairs lined the far wall. All empty. A stack of papers and a few pencils sat in the middle of the table.

Mark separated from Kristy to give himself some room. If he didn't do something soon, he wouldn't get the chance.

Carl yanked a chair out and shoved it towards Mark. "Sit." The gun was trained on his chest.

Mark rounded the chair, bringing him closer to Carl. He sank partway into the chair, then exploded at Carl, keeping low. His shoulder caught Carl in the stomach. The man grunted, and they fell together. The gun blast echoed off the walls. Mark hoped it hadn't changed trajectory.

He yanked the weapon from Carl's hand and propelled it across the room. "Kristy, get the gun." He'd tossed it far enough that she wouldn't get mixed up in his battle with Carl. He punched the man in the face and flipped him to his stomach. Holding him down with a knee to the spine, Mark extracted a zip-tie from his pocket and bound the man's wrists. He stood and yanked Carl to his feet.

Kristy held up the gun, dangling from a trembling finger. Her voice was tight, barely above a whisper. "Mark, do you want this?"

"No. You hold onto it for now."

Mark prodded Carl. "Get moving. We're going outside." He kept a grip on the man's upper arm.

"You won't get away with this. You don't know where we've got our people."

In this instance, there was safety in numbers. "You mean, like the policeman who persuaded us to come here? I'm sure we'll find some honest people."

Mark dialed the emergency number. "I need a couple of police cars at Freeland Enterprises. We just freed ourselves from a kidnapping."

"Kidnapping?" the dispatcher said. "Are you in a safe place now?"

"I've got them tied up. Can you tell the officers who responded to the Dalton property that Kristy Collins is here?"

"Oh. We've already been notified by Jason Ballard. Officers are en route."

"Thanks." Mark ended the call. "Kristy, can you hold the door open?"

She raced ahead and stayed behind the door as he passed through with Gretsky. He shivered as the slimy ants left his skin. Mark nodded at Jason, who leaned against the hood of his car. He wasn't surprised to find his friend waiting. "Good to see you, Jason."

Mark looped his foot around Carl's ankles and shoved him into the grass. The man should be happy Mark hadn't dropped him on the sidewalk. Once he was down, Mark zip-tied the man's ankles.

Mark waved toward the man on the ground and glanced at Jason. "Keep an eye on him. I have to go back in." Not that he wanted the slime again, but he couldn't chance the police going in to get the other officer and falling under the spell.

He gave Kristy a quick kiss on his way past, steeling himself for the slime, then retrieved the officer that he'd hidden in a nearby room. The officer had maneuvered himself into a sitting position. Mark cut the tie from the man's ankles and yanked him to his feet. "Your buddies are coming for you. I'm sure they won't be happy when they find out you're a dirty cop."

"I didn't have a choice."

"Yeah, right."

Once more through the door and getting rid of the creeping ants, Mark dropped the man beside Carl.

Two police cars flew up the road and into the parking lot. Lights flashing and sirens blaring, they stopped behind the parked cars. The sirens died, but the blue and white lights bathed the scene. The officers joined the small group. The first one nodded at the uniformed officer on the ground. "Hey, what's Riley doing tied up?"

Mark grabbed Kristy's hand and once she was close enough, wrapped his arm around her waist. "He kidnapped Kristy and me and brought us here."

The man nudged Riley's knee. "Riley, what's up with that?"

"I didn't do it. They overpowered me and kidnapped me."

Mark chuckled. "Yeah. That explains why I called the police."

Kristy snuggled closer and dropped her head to his shoulder. He glanced down to find her eyes closed. He was used to keeping late hours when needed, but the stress of being kidnapped a second time probably had done her in.

Mark rubbed Kristy's back. "Look, can we give statements tomorrow? This has been exhausting."

Three officers' eyes zeroed in on Kristy. The senior

officer said, "Sorry, sir. Since this involves one of our officers, you'll have to give statements now. You can follow me in, and the other units will follow."

Mark covered a yawn and gazed at the lead officer. It would be a long while before they slept.

Mark and Kristy got into the back of Jason's SUV. "Sorry, you can't get home to Shauna and the baby."

"Couldn't be helped. Let's hope we got the top guys tonight." Jason pulled onto the road behind the lead police cruiser.

Kristy lifted the medallion. "Can I take this off now?"

"Yes," Mark said.

She pulled it over her head, dropped it into his palm, and he slipped it into his jacket pocket.

They were separated at the station and it took a couple of hours to answer all the questions. Kristy finished last since she'd been kidnapped earlier.

Mark, in the entry waiting area with Jason, stood as Kristy came out of the interview room, and he wrapped an arm around her. He looked at Jason. "It's too late to drive all the way home now. How about finishing the night here and leaving in the morning?"

"Good idea."

On the walk back to the car, Mark scrolled through his phone on a search for motels. "I'll find something. If that policeman was part of this group, anyone could be. I'll look for a chain, so we can hide the car in a full parking lot." He gave directions.

Chapter 16

Kristy woke in a warm cocoon of Mark's embrace. She didn't know what time they'd gotten to their hotel room, but she'd stripped and crashed on the bed, and Mark had joined her minutes later. With his arms around her, dreamless sleep had claimed her.

Soft lips touched her temple. "G'morning."

She snuggled closer and kissed his neck. "It's so nice, and...safe to wake up like this." They'd barely shared a bed before she'd been taken. She missed everything about him, but what she needed this moment was the physical closeness. And he was so good at it.

She ran her palm up his side, then lightly scratched her nails down his back. His body responded just the way she wanted it to. She peppered kisses up his throat, over his chin and to his lips. "I have this Mark orgasm deficit. I think you're the only one who can fix it."

He grinned. "I think you're right." His lips roamed lower and lower with breathtaking stops along the way.

She ran her fingers through his hair and held his head to her when he stopped at her most sensitive spot. She gasped. While his mouth worked its magic, his hands found other places to tease.

Before Mark, this would have been simply two bodies fulfilling their need for sexual gratification. That's all she'd known, and it was hollow and shallow, compared to the love now seeping into her heart and soul.

Waves, like a stormy sea rolled over her, flooding her senses with so much pleasure. But it wasn't enough. She tugged Mark's arms, and he surged over her. His lips met hers, sharing her flavor. She rolled them over and straddled him, then took him into her. She kissed him as they found a rhythm.

As her peak approached, she tipped her head back so she could watch him. Their gazes held and he shifted, changing the angle, sending her over the edge. As he followed with his own release, she caught the possessive glow in his eyes before she closed hers to luxuriate in the full body climax.

Kristy collapsed on top of Mark. "Wow. That was..." She blew out a long breath, willing her heart to slow.

Mark kissed her. "Love. That was love." He brushed her hair behind her ear, revealing a strange mark on his palm.

She grabbed his wrist and touched the spot. "What's this?"

He looped his other arm around her, and showed Kristy his other palm. "I have a matched set."

She rubbed a finger over the smooth, white skin on his hand. "It's a burn." She frowned. "How did you get matching burns?"

"I had to hold that pendulum while it was hot and recite the find spell. Twice."

Her heart, which had calmed, sped up again. "You did magic for me?" She kissed his palm. "You burned yourself to find me." She groped behind her. "Give me your other hand."

His fingers took hers, and she kissed the mark on his palm. The first time, he might not have known how much it would hurt, but repeating the spell, he knew what would happen. He'd suffered to get her back.

Tears filled her eyes, and she blinked, one spilling down

her cheek. If she didn't know before how much Mark loved her, this demonstrated it in the most graphic way. "I love you. I'm not walking away from you this time."

Mark's phone on the night table rang. He gave her a quick kiss. "And I'd do everything I could think of to convince you to stay if you tried." He snatched up the phone. "Hey, Jason." His gaze flicked to the clock. "I didn't realize it was that late. Okay, we'll meet you there in twenty minutes."

He hung up the phone and tapped her hip. "We're meeting Jason in the hotel restaurant. He's anxious to get back home."

Kristy scooted off the bed and headed to the bathroom. That wasn't much time, but how much time would she need when she didn't have to choose her clothes or put on makeup? Her bra hung over the shower rod. She'd forgotten about it, but Mark hadn't. She grabbed the clothing and dropped it on the counter beside a comb and two wrapped toothbrushes. Her man was thoughtful.

***

Mark held Kristy's hand on his thigh. He hadn't been able to release her for long since getting her back, and he didn't care that Jason sat in the front seat alone. "I'm not surprised Harrison, Terrence, and Carl got out on bail. And we still didn't find out who the other guy was that kidnapped Kristy."

Jason met his gaze in the mirror. "It's too bad about the cop, though."

Kristy pressed against Mark's arm. She'd been upset when Mark had called the police station in the morning to make sure there weren't any more question before they left and heard about the officer. "I know he was a policeman, and the other officers were probably pretty hard on him, but do you guys think he really committed suicide?"

Mark squeezed her hand. "No. Two suicides of men in jail who are associated with Harrison Dalton are too much of a coincidence. Besides, he left a pregnant wife behind."

Kristy's eyes widened, and he wished he could have kept her in the dark. "That poor woman. Because of Harrison, she'll have to raise her baby alone. Who's the other?"

"The man who tried to kidnap you from the driveway."

"How come I didn't know about that?"

Mark stared out the window. "We weren't exactly on speaking terms when I found out. And later, I didn't think about it."

"But—"

He kissed her. Mark couldn't believe he was using a kiss as a tactic to stop her question. Jason chuckled, and he ignored it. Her hand touched Mark's neck and slipped into his hair. He loved the way her fingers curled, her nails gently scraping his scalp.

He tipped his head back and she sighed.

"Shauna and Tony collected your stuff from my parents' house," Jason said. "My parents are coming home tomorrow. We thought you'd be more comfortable at our place than with them."

Mark rubbed Kristy's arm. "It's probably not a good idea with Harrison and Carl back on the street. They have even more reason to use this spell since they'll want to sweep this kidnapping charge under the mat."

"They're probably getting reorganized. One night shouldn't hurt."

"We need to end this. They'll keep coming after Kristy, unless they find someone else to solve the puzzle. And that's bad for everybody. That spell needs to disappear, but there are copies of it all over, and we don't know where the original is."

Kristy sat straighter, and stared at Jason's back. "It'd be nice if there was some kind of magic to make all the copies of the spell burn up or disappear from hard drives."

Jason shook his head. "I can't think of how that could be done. The best we can do is put those guys into prison."

They passed the welcome sign for Rawlins. Maybe this would be a nice place for Kristy and him to find a home. Their best friends living here was the best incentive. But it wasn't something that could be decided now, and they'd have to work it out together.

Kristy yawned, and rested her head on Mark's shoulder.

"It's been a long day," Mark said. "Let's give it some thought and throw ideas around in the morning."

They couldn't hide out forever. He'd find a way to resolve this without giving in to Harrison.

***

Mark pulled on a t-shirt. Kristy came out of the bathroom wrapped in a towel. He would have preferred if she'd left it behind, but the bitten lip and silver packet she stared at concerned him.

"Baby, what's the matter?"

She flipped the packet around. Pills.

"I haven't taken my birth control pills for three days."

Protection hadn't crossed his mind since she was on birth control. "Does that mean you could be pregnant?"

She shrugged. "Maybe."

He held in his grin, waiting to see her response.

"If I take the missed doses…"

"What?"

"It might cause birth defects or mis—"

He snatched the package out of her hand and dropped it

into the trash. He already wanted to protect the possible new life. The thought of them having a child completed a picture for him. He'd imagined a baby in Kristy's arms and him holding both of them.

He sat with her on the bed. "I see three options. We use condoms and start birth control if you're not pregnant. Or if you are pregnant, we don't need condoms anymore." He grinned. "Or we don't use condoms. You're pregnant, or you will be soon enough." He should probably let her choose from all the options, although he didn't like this one. "And there's the morning after pill."

Her mouth dropped open. "You're not upset?"

He kissed the ring on her finger, then flipped her hand and kissed her palm. "Baby, I asked you to marry me because I love you, and I want the whole package. A baby sooner than later is fine with me."

She threw her arms around his neck and buried her face. "I was in shock for a couple of minutes when I realized I could be pregnant."

He slid his hand under the flap of her towel and rested it on her stomach. Even now, a tiny speck of cells might be multiplying into a baby.

She rocked her head. "I didn't think I wanted children but helping Shauna with Logan made me see that maybe I do." She leaned back, and he was mesmerized by her bright eyes. "I don't want a token child."

He frowned, not able to grasp her meaning. "Token?"

"That's what I always felt like. "Dad wanted children, and Mom decided to give him one. Me. A token." She bit her lip. "So, if we're doing this, we're having more than one, because I don't want my child to feel like a token."

He cupped her cheek. Even now, after all she'd worked through, there were still reservations about who she was. "You are not a token. Your dad loves you, and that's what's important. If we have only one, our child will not be a token. We'll both love him or her." He smiled. "But I don't mind if we have more." He rubbed her cheek. "What's your decision?"

"You want me to decide?"

"It's your body." He hoped he'd given her enough of a clue what he wanted without forcing her to give in to his wishes. If there'd been a right time before to discuss children, he would have gone all out with enthusiasm.

She stared at him, and he was afraid she'd say she needed more time, and he'd have to give it to her. He hoped her decision was the same as his.

She maintained eye contact and slipped her hands to either side of his face. A myriad of emotions flashed across her face. "No condoms. No pills."

He gave a whoop and tipped back with her.

She giggled. "What are you doing?"

"I thought I'd increase our chances of getting pregnant."

***

Kristy rested her hand on Mark's arm. Shauna and Jason sat across from her at the dining room table. Mark rubbed Logan's back as the baby turned his head to stare at Kristy. The sleepy little eyes blinked but maintained eye contact. She couldn't resist stroking his soft hair. It surprised her how much she loved this little guy.

She turned back to the table, and caught Shauna sliding a glance at Mark, then studying her. Her friend was going to ask her about them having babies. "So, how do we stop the bad guys?"

Mark put the baby into his little bed behind Shauna, and covered him with a blanket. He was going to make a terrific father.

Mark sat beside Kristy and took her hand. "Even if you don't give them the cryptogram solution, eventually, they'll find someone who can. It would be nice to get the original and all copies of it."

Kristy threw up the hand Mark wasn't holding. "But it's everywhere! Even at the Freeland office, my partial solution was on the table in the conference room. Someone must have emailed it there from Harrison's house. So, that's on at least two computers. It's on that fake cryptogram website, and who knows where else. And how could we possibly find the original?"

It was impossible. They'd always be after her, and she might be pregnant. That was no kind of life for children with it hanging over their heads.

"If we put the top people involved in prison for kidnapping, that should slow them down," Jason said.

Kristy huffed. "Slow down. Not stop. If Harrison ends up in prison, he'll have teams of people on the outside trying to figure out the solution so he can use the spell to get released."

Mark leaned his elbows on the table. "There's always arson to get rid of the original."

"What!" Kristy swatted his arm. "You're not risking prison by burning down Harrison's house."

"Hey. I could do it without getting caught. But I was only kidding. The spell is probably in a fireproof safe." Mark whooshed out a breath. "Which means I'm going back into that house."

That didn't sound good. At all. Harrison was back home. That meant he had bodyguards and probably lots of other security. Kristy bit her lip. "Aren't home safes usually hidden? How can you find one in that huge house? It'd be like searching for a lost necklace at a county fair."

Shauna chuckled, probably remembering how long

they'd hunted for the necklace Kristy's father had given her for her sixteenth birthday. And they never found it.

Mark narrowed his eyes. "There's a story there. So, Harrison's house. We can eliminate about eighty-percent of it. He might have a safe in his bedroom, but not any others. It won't be in the kitchen since staff would be there more often than not. His office is the most likely place since it's the most convenient. There could be a second safe in the basement."

"I'll come along," Jason said.

"What I'd like you to do is go to Freeland Enterprises, wipe Carl's computer and find those pages that Kristy saw." He wished he'd grabbed them while they were there.

Jason's hands shot up. "I'm not going back in there."

Mark grinned and extracted the policeman's chain from his pocket. "I've got this for you. That cop had it on him and the enhanced protection spell didn't affect him. I put it on Kristy, and the zombie effect faded, so I know it works." He tossed it to Jason, who caught it and dropped it over his head.

"I'm taking down the fake website before we leave," Mark said. "And I'll remove anything associated with it from Kristy's tablet."

Jason leaned with his forearms on the table. "Okay. So, when do we go and what do we do with Kristy?"

Kristy couldn't stay at Shauna's. She'd likely been tracked by her phone or tablet the first time, but it couldn't have been how they'd found her at Jason's parents' house. Chances were they'd find her again.

Mark rubbed her thigh. "I called Zack and Trey last night. They'll be here shortly. I'm having them take Kristy to a motel to guard her there."

Kristy could take her tablet, but she couldn't ignore the guys the whole time. "Shauna, do you have a deck of cards?"

Mark shook his head. "I'm going to have to warn them not to bet money with you."

Kristy giggled. One day at *Pirates' Cove*, they'd played poker, and she'd cleaned him out of his cash.

Mark took Kristy's hand. "Let's hope we can get rid of all copies of the spell. Otherwise, I'm at a loss what to do to protect you, honey."

Chapter 17

Mark sat at the wheel of his SUV, facing the car rental office door. He'd had Zack wipe out the fake website, and Mark had cleared every bit of puzzle data from Kristy's tablet.

It had been hard to leave Kristy when he remembered what happened the last time he'd left her. This time though, he had men he'd worked with for years—men he could trust with his life—guarding her. They'd scowled when introduced to Kristy, and shown surprise when she'd kissed him and told him to be careful. He hadn't realized his breakup with her had left his emotions so raw that his men had noticed.

Jason strode out, tossing and catching the keys to the car he'd rented. He got into a black Toyota Corolla, and Mark followed him onto the street. Four blocks up, they turned into a discount department store's parking lot and parked near the road. They met behind the cars.

Mark checked his watch. "We're about twenty minutes from both targets. Keep your phone on silent. Send a text after completing your mission. We'll meet back here. If one of us doesn't return by twenty-two-hundred, the other will assume a capture and go in for a rescue, Got your location?" Two hours would be more than enough time for Jason.

Jason tapped his temple. "Memorized." Jason had asked Sheila where in the building Carl's office was located. One plus in their favor—it was on the first floor. They'd checked floor plans and plotted the best route.

"Still got the necklace?"

Jason rubbed his chest. "Yes."

"Ski mask?"

Jason patted his jacket pocket.

Mark held out his hand, and Jason clasped it. "Good luck, man. And thanks for doing this."

"Hey, just returning the favor for what you did to get my sister back."

Mark couldn't help but think that this was more dangerous than Jamie's rescue. They'd had six men attacking that building, but he and Jason were sneaking in separately.

They got in the cars and headed in opposite directions. They'd done a preliminary perimeter check at Harrison's house and discovered that the ladder they'd left on the ground, inside next to the fence, was still there. Mark had purchased another ladder for use on the outside of the fence.

He parked in the same spot they'd used before—off the road and under some trees. He donned the gloves, ski mask, and night vision goggles. As quiet as possible, he removed the ladder from the back and unfolded it, then carried it to the trail near the fence.

This time, he'd chosen a spot near the back corner to scale the fence, reducing the likelihood of discovery as it was left in place. He made a sweep with the goggles.

He climbed, teetered on the top edge of the fence between the spikes, then dropped over the side, landing with bent knees. He straightened the goggles, pulled out his gun, and stayed low as he raced for the nearest tree. His heart pounded, and he waited as his breathing slowed. The last time, they must have been observed since Terrence had taken Kristy from her room. He couldn't believe it was a coincidence. He hoped there were no cameras at the back of the house.

Another peek, then he ran for the house, plastering his back to the wall, and slipped behind an air conditioning unit. On this mission, the best entrance was through the basement. The yard sloped to a walk-out metal door without windows. He assumed there would be a silent alarm when he breached the door, but hoped there'd be no more than one guard at a time.

Mark holstered his gun and withdrew his lock picks. The lock yielded in thirty-eight seconds. He exchanged the picks for his gun, pushed up his goggles and cracked the door, listening before opening it farther. A rhythmic clang of metal alternated with a huffed breath. There must be an exercise room nearby. He stepped through the door, closed it, and swept his gun across the space. He stood in a corridor with doorways on both sides—some open and others closed.

On silent feet, Mark followed the clang to the third doorway on the left. Inside, he spied one man, his back to him, standing in front of a weight machine, probably pulling about a hundred-twenty pounds. He could continue to the first floor and hope this man didn't do a sweep of the building once finished exercising. But Mark risked being the one taken by surprise.

He grabbed a ten-pound free weight as he passed a rack and swung it at the guy's head. The man released the bar with a clang of weights and stumbled to the side. The guy spun around, and Mark threw the weight at him. As the man reached for it, Mark jumped on him, dropping him to the floor. A couple of quick face punches disoriented him enough for Mark to zip-tie his hands. He ripped off a piece of duct tape and slapped it across the man's mouth. That would be fun to remove from the beard and mustache. After zip-tying the man's ankles, Mark dragged him to the wall next to the door to hide him from immediate discovery.

Mark waited beside the door, listening. Quiet. He stuck his head out, finding the corridor empty. Normally, he'd search all the rooms, but due to time constraints, he only checked the ones with open doors as he worked his way to the stairs. He hoped that decision wouldn't haunt him later.

At the stair alcove, he slipped around the corner and crept up the steps, pausing on the landing before the door. He drew in a deep breath and blew it out slowly. The last time he'd slunk through a house in a search, it'd been a drug lord's home on the edge of a jungle. He and the three guys with him had carried AR-15s as well as their holstered handguns of choice. Back then, he'd had nothing to go home to. He hadn't intentionally thrown himself into danger, but knowing no one would miss him had given him an edge. Now, he wanted to get this done and go home to Kristy.

Mark cracked the door, listened, then pulled it open far enough to check each direction. Empty. Again, he skulked down the corridor and checked the rooms with open doors, wishing he had time to be more thorough. He stepped into a room with an empty desk—no computer or laptop. No safes hid behind pictures or in the closet.

In the next room, a laptop sat on the desk. Mark holstered his gun. He inserted a flash drive into the computer and turned it on. As it booted from his drive, he searched for a safe. Nothing. He returned to the laptop, and installed a program to overwrite the hard drive. Once that was running, he removed his thumb drive and headed to the next room.

It was another office. How many were in this place? He inserted his drive in the tower under the desk and turned on the computer, then checked the folders in the desk basket. One folder contained information on Kristy, and he pocketed it.

Mark peeked behind a painting. *Got it!* He set the picture on the floor and examined the safe. *Yes!* An electronic lock.

He withdrew a small box with a screen from his pocket, punched in some settings and taped it beside the keypad. Then he started his overwriting program on the computer.

Mark picked a lock on the desk and searched the drawers for Kristy's puzzle work. Inside a folder in the bottom right drawer were five sheets with Kristy's writing on them. He folded up the papers and stuffed them into his pocket, then returned the folder to the drawer.

A check of the monitor found that the program was running. He removed his flash drive, and examined the safecracking device—not finished yet.

He peeked out the door and found the corridor empty. It didn't make sense. He figured he'd run into security on this level, or at least residents. Maybe after the police had released him, Harrison had fled.

Back in the room, Mark was relieved to find the device on the safe had finished. He twisted the handle and opened the door. He examined the first paper and flipped it face-down on a nearby table. The next was a small book, and he leafed through the pages—no spells, no inserted pages. He flipped it on top of the first sheet. The fifth item in the safe was a spell book, and at least fifty years old. Most of the spells were not encrypted, likely leaving the most dangerous ones hard to use. He hesitated tearing the one spell out of the book, and decided to take the whole book, slipping it into his pocket.

Mark flipped the contents he'd removed and set them back inside the safe. He closed and reset the lock then covered it with the painting.

He left the building the way he'd entered and jogged to the fence. He had the ladder erected, climbed it, and jumped to the ground in less than a minute. He raced for his car, flipped up his ski mask, and got on the road. Missions almost never went as planned. Usually, more obstacles blocked the completion. This was one of the easiest he'd ever done. And he didn't like it.

A few blocks away, he pulled over and sent a text to Jason, noting that Jason hadn't sent his own text yet. *Done.*

Mark's job had been shorter than expected, but Jason's should have been half the time. It worried him. He approached the parking lot but didn't see Jason's rental. Nine-thirty-three. *Screw it.* He kept driving.

He slowed as he passed Freeland Enterprises. A lone car was parked near the door. About a half-mile up, parked half off the road, was Jason's rental. He'd hoped Jason had been delayed and they'd missed each other on the road.

Mark made a u-turn, and entered the parking lot, rolling into a space one away from the other vehicle. He covered his face and left the car. He checked the entrance door and found it unlocked, like a big neon sign saying 'Welcome.'

He plunged through the doorway and shivered, hating the slimy ant crawls. He paused and listened. Nothing. The route to Carl's office was in the opposite direction he'd gone last time. He hurried to the turn in the hallway and peeked around the corner. Empty.

With stealthy steps, he worked his way down the hall. Most office doors were closed, the small windows in the doors black. Light from one doorway blended into the hallway light. Based on Sheila's directions, that was Carl's office.

"Where is she?" Carl's voice.

"I don't know who you're talking about." Flesh pounding flesh was accompanied by Jason's grunt. Mark wished they could trade places. He hated that his friend suffered for helping him.

"You were here with Kristy when I was arrested."

"Oh, you mean that pretty woman with the wavy, blonde hair? First time I ever saw her."

184

Mark reached the door and peeked in. Jason sat in a chair, his hands behind him. His lip was cut, and blood covered the top of his shoulder. A flicker in his eyes showed he'd noticed Mark.

Carl leaned close to Jason. "How about the pretty woman named Shauna? I sent a couple of men to bring Kristy back. They don't mind messing her up a little to get what they want."

Jason's face filled with rage. "Leave her out of this."

It was a good thing they'd planned for this possibility. Shauna and Logan had been dropped at the Ballards' on the way out of town. She had Reese, Tony, and Jamie's husband, Theron, to keep her safe. Unless Carl's men were something special, three against two should be enough.

Mark stepped into the room, his gun targeted on Carl. "It's over."

Carl spun around and stepped behind Jason. He yanked a knife from his pocket, flipped it open and held it near Jason's throat. "It doesn't look over to me. I want Kristy or this man dies."

Heat rose in his chest. "You're never again getting your hands on her." This wouldn't help Jason. He needed to get back on mission. He tamped down his worry and willed his heart to calm.

Jason's body was no shield while sitting, with most of Carl's chest exposed.

Mark squeezed the trigger. The roar echoed in the small room at the same time red bloomed just above Carl's elbow. The man groaned and clutched his wound, dropping the knife into Jason's lap, fortunately, not point down. Jason thrust his chair back, knocking Carl into the wall.

Mark darted forward and shoved Carl to the floor. He zip-tied the man's wrists, not at all sorry for Carl's yelp of pain.

Mark fished his knife from his pocket and released Jason from the tape on his wrists.

"You won't get away with this," Carl yelled. "I've got friends in the police department. I've got a judge on my payroll."

Jason stood and let the knife drop to the floor. He yanked off the remaining tape and rubbed his wrists.

Mark kicked Carl's ankle. "Yeah? The charges didn't get dropped." He patted Jason's non-bloodied shoulder. "You okay, man?"

"I've been better. Been worse, too."

Mark talked over Carl's ranting. "What about that shoulder?"

Jason glanced at the bloody spot. "It's fine. Carl stabbed me with a pen. Didn't go deep. I wiped the computer but didn't have time to search for the papers."

"Drag him outside while I finish the search. Give me ten minutes before calling the police." The police couldn't enter the door, or they'd probably follow Carl's directions, and arrest Jason and Mark.

"I got it." Jason swept up his ski mask from the floor and shoved it into an oversized pocket on his thigh. He yanked Carl to his feet, and led him from the room, his tirade waning.

Mark didn't know if Jason had picked the lock or if he'd walked in like Mark, but he could be held for breaking and entering. Of course, Jason being questioned and beaten wasn't a necessary part of containment.

Mark removed his ski mask and jammed it into a pocket. Carl already knew who he was. Hopefully, the police wouldn't frisk him and find it.

Mark searched the desk drawers. Nothing. He noticed Jason's flash drive still in the laptop and grabbed it.

He yanked open the top drawer of the filing cabinet

behind the desk and checked inside the first folder, then read all the headings. Nothing fit. He searched each drawer and slammed the last one closed. He paced along the edges of the room, inspecting anything that might hide the sheets. A door he'd passed had been labeled *Security*. Maybe Carl had hidden the pages there.

The police would arrive soon, and he needed to find the spell before then, or he'd never get it. He raced down the hall to the security room and found the door locked. With his pick, the door was open in thirty seconds flat. He stepped in and flipped on the lights. A desk faced a wall with four monitors displaying views of rooms and corridors, cycling through new locations every few seconds.

Mark searched drawers and sifted through the contents of an in-basket tray. He bumped the keyboard as he straightened, and the edge of a paper peeked out. Lifting aside the keyboard, he snatched up the papers and unfolded them.

"Yes!" He stuffed the spell sheets into his pocket, turned out the light, and closed the door. He made his way outside. Relief from the slimy ants, finally.

Jason sat on the hood of Carl's car, phone to his ear, while Carl glared at him. "I'll call you later. Bye, honey."

"Shauna's okay?"

Jason grinned. "Yes." He kicked a foot toward Carl. "His guys showed up at Mom and Dad's and got themselves arrested."

Some of the tension left Mark's shoulders. Those men wouldn't be going after Kristy.

A police unit with lights but no siren turned in and stopped behind both cars. Two officers got out. The first one to reach them put his hands on his hips. "We were here a couple of days ago." He squinted at Carl. "Didn't we arrest you?"

Carl squirmed to a sitting position. "I was released on bail." He nodded toward Jason and Mark. "These men should be arrested for breaking and entering."

Mark pointed to the door. "The door was unlocked when I got here. I headed straight to Carl's office where I found my friend tied to a chair and being beaten by Carl. When he saw me, he held a knife to Jason's throat. That's when I winged him."

"It was unlocked when I got here, too," Jason said.

Carl bristled. "You were riffling through my drawers when I entered my office."

Jason shrugged. "I got bored."

The officers' gazes had ping-ponged between them. "Where's the knife?" the first one asked.

Mark pointed behind him. "It's on the floor in Carl's office."

The officer collected a plastic bag and glove from his pocket. "I'll retrieve it."

Mark held up his hand. "Hold on. Jason, can I have the medallion?"

Jason removed it and tossed it to Mark.

Mark held the necklace out to the officer. "You have to wear this. It's...got a chip in it to prevent the security system from incapacitating you."

The man narrowed his eyes. "Are you serious? I've never heard of such a thing."

"Ask Jason. The first time he entered without that necklace, his head hurt so bad he thought it would explode."

The cop inspected the medallion, shrugged and dropped it over his head. "Lead the way."

Mark took him to Carl's office and pointed at the knife on the floor. Next to it was the discarded duct tape that had been wrapped around Jason's wrists.

The man slipped on the glove, picked up the knife and

dropped it into the bag, sealing it shut. He took out another bag and stuffed the duct tape inside. Mark guessed he'd want to check DNA to find out if Jason really was the one tied up.

The officer patted the medallion. "So, if I took this off, I'd be hit with a headache from hell?"

"No. You only need that to get through the door. Once you're inside, you're fine."

"What about the employees? Do they all wear these?"

"I'm guessing they only turn on the field after hours." Mark gestured at the door. "Ready to leave?"

The cop scanned the room, pausing at the chair in the middle and nodded. "Let's go."

They went back outside. Carl was standing with the other officer's hand grasping his arm. The first officer lifted the necklace.

"No. Keep it. You may have to go back in." Mark glared at Carl. "Hey, Carl. Does your security automatically turn off by morning?" Mark couldn't imagine the turmoil if the employees passed through the door and like zombies, headed to Carl's office. Then someone would have to hand out painkillers like Halloween candy.

Carl pursed his lips.

Mark took a step closer. "Answer me."

"Yes. It turns off at five."

The officer holding Carl shuffled him toward the police car.

The first officer met Mark's gaze. "I need the two of you to come in and give statements."

Carl squirmed. "Why aren't you taking them in? You're trusting them to show up?"

The cop closest to Carl nodded toward Jason. "He's the one who called the police. If you were so worried about a B and E, you would have called. And you're out on bail. The judge may want to rescind that."

189

"See you in a few," Jason said.

The police car drove away, and Mark said, "I sure hope this is almost over."

Chapter 18

Mark pulled into Jason's driveway and rubbed his face. It had been a long night. Shauna's car sat in the driveway, and he was overjoyed to see Zack's rental, which meant his life would be perfect with Kristy back in his arms.

Jason had slept on the way back. At least one of them would be refreshed. Mark smacked him in the arm. "We're home."

Jason stretched and groaned. "Thanks for driving."

Mark followed Jason into the house. Group laughter came from the kitchen. His gaze immediately found Kristy, her eyes sparkling with merriment.

Her eyes widened. "Mark!" She flew across the room, nearly knocking him over when she slammed into him.

He wrapped his arms around her and spun in a full circle. His lips claimed hers. It had been less than twenty hours since their last kiss, but it felt like weeks. He squeezed her tight for a moment longer and tipped his head back. "I missed you."

"Me, too. Come eat breakfast." She dragged him to the table and pushed him into the chair beside the one she'd occupied. "I'll get you some coffee. Grab some food."

He gave a nod to Zack and Trey. "Thanks for keeping Kristy safe." Then loaded his plate with scrambled eggs, bacon and fried potatoes.

Kristy set full cups on the table for Jason and him, then kissed Mark's cheek and took her seat.

Shauna gently kissed Jason's split lip. "What happened?" She dragged him to the table and filled a plate for him.

Jason touched the corner of his lip. "It turned out I had the harder job."

"Carl did that?" Shauna asked.

Mark shrugged off his jacket. "Yeah. And it would have been worse if I hadn't gotten there when I did." He didn't want to think about what condition Jason would have been in if Mark had waited until the agreed upon time.

Mark emptied his coat pockets onto the table and draped his coat over the chair back.

Kristy opened one of the folded sheets and then the next. "You found them." She picked up the book. "What's this?"

"A spell book. Besides your spell, there are a couple more encrypted ones in there. And a few that aren't." He caught Jason's eye. "I thought your mom should take the book."

Jason nodded. "Good idea."

Kristy stared at a page with mixed up letters. He took the book from her hands and closed it on the table. "Don't even think about it."

"I-but I loved the challenge. It was the most fun ever."

He whispered in her ear. "Ever?"

She grinned and whispered back. "A different kind of fun. You can't compare them."

Mark wolfed down his food. Being up all night sure made a guy hungry for breakfast. He gave a side eye to Kristy. And being away from her for a full day made a guy hungry for her kind of fun. He pushed the empty plate away and leaned back. "Let me catch you up on everything."

He told them about going to Harrison's house and

finding only one bodyguard.

Kristy scooted her chair closer to Mark and leaned against him. "I wonder if Harrison skipped the country and took his staff with him."

Mark wrapped an arm around her shoulders and kissed her temple. "I'll get to that."

He gazed at Jason. His friend had certainly gotten the worst of it. "I finished early and figured I'd check on Jason. Carl had him tied up and was punching him."

Shauna gasped.

She grabbed Jason's t-shirt. "Let me see your ribs."

He held her hands. "They're fine."

She glared. "Let me see."

"Fine." He leaned close to her and whispered, but Mark heard it. "But I get to see under your shirt later."

Mark chuckled at Shauna's blush. Jason lifted his t-shirt, and lucky for him no bruises showed. Shauna kissed his cheek. "Okay, Mark. Continue."

"So, anyway, Carl was put back in jail for assaulting Jason. He's going before the judge today see if they'll revoke bail. While we were giving our statements, we heard that Harrison and his bodyguard had been in an accident."

Kristy raised her brows. "Is that why he wasn't at the house when you were there?"

"I think so. His car was t-boned not far from his house and launched over an embankment. It rolled a couple of times. The car that hit him followed it over, which made it worse."

Kristy snuggled closer to him. "How bad was it?"

"The bodyguard should get out of the hospital in a couple of days. Harrison died in surgery."

Her eyes widened. "Harrison is dead?"

"I can't say I'm unhappy about his death." He ran his hand into Kristy's hair at the back of her neck. "He can't come after you again."

She relaxed against him. "Wow. It's over."

"That sounds like a pretty vicious attack," Zack said. "Who did it?"

"Remember the police officer who kidnapped Kristy and me and then died in jail?"

He received various forms of assent. "His wife did it. I think she knew Harrison had her husband killed."

Kristy frowned. "But wasn't she pregnant?"

Mark nodded. "She was rushed to the hospital. Her baby was born by c-section before she died."

Kristy squeezed his arm. "She must have been crazy with grief to risk herself and her unborn child like that. Is he okay?"

"She's a month early, but her chances are good."

"She was born an orphan. Does she have anyone?"

Mark was warmed that Kristy cared so much for this baby's loss. "The mother's sister and her husband have two kids. They're going to take her."

"I'm glad she has family."

Mark rubbed his temples. His head pounded. He didn't do all-nighters as easily as he used to. He grasped Kristy's hand and stood. "I'm going to bed."

Kristy's eyes narrowed, and she stood. Her fingertips kneaded his temples. "Do you want a massage?"

"You give massages?"

She took his hand and pulled him toward the stairs. "I took a six-week course. I'm not a masseuse, but I can make you feel good."

The men behind him laughed.

"Why didn't you tell us last night you could give massages?" Trey said.

Mark yelled over his shoulder. "She's not touching anybody except me." Kristy could make him feel great with just a glance, but a relaxing massage sounded perfect.

***

The next day, Mark had asked Shauna to take Kristy shopping. She didn't need much convincing. He drove to Jason's office using his GPS.

The free-standing building was as respectable as the others on the street. He parked in a lot shared with the next building.

Through the glass front door, a dark-skinned woman sat at a desk, a phone headset on her head. She typed on a keyboard in front of her, although her monitor was shifted to the side. The receptionist met his gaze and smiled.

He opened the door and entered but stopped just inside, giving her a modicum of privacy. Her voice changed as she started wrapping up. He could see why Jason hired her. That mellow voice would calm the most distressed client.

The phone dropped into its cradle. "How can I help you?" One hand rested on the desk—blood red nails, moderate length.

"I'd like to see Jason."

"He's with a client. Should be done in ten minutes or so."

"I'll wait. I'm staying with him, but—"

Her dark eyes widened. "You're Mark? Super spy?"

He chuckled. "Not actually a spy."

"I'm Alicia. You're the reason he has a cut lip and bruised jaw." Obviously, she cared about her boss.

Mark shrugged. "Sometimes it can't be avoided. What he did for me helped save my fiancée's life." He grinned. "So we're even. A couple years ago, I helped him save *his* fiancée. Of course, I didn't get punched in the face."

She laughed and waved a hand toward a coffee station.

195

"Why don't you get coffee and take a seat?"

"Thanks." Six forest green, ceramic mugs sat upside-down on a cloth-covered tray beside a single-cup coffee maker. Jason was doing a good job creating a high-end agency. He filled a cup and sat in the middle of a leather couch the same color as the cups. Two matching easy chairs hugged the adjoining wall. He ignored the magazines on the coffee table and checked messages on his phone.

Voices drew Mark's attention. Jason raised his brows but continued talking to an older man as he escorted him to the door. After the man left, Jason strode to the couch and Mark stood.

Jason tucked a thumb in his pocket. "What are you doing here? You could have called."

"I wanted to check the place out. It's impressive."

"Thanks. Let me show you around." He stopped in front of Alicia. "I assume you two have met. Alicia August, best office assistant ever, meet my best friend, Mark Simmons."

She laughed. "Don't let Shauna hear you say that."

"She said it first. She'd rather stick to accounting. And between my business and Dad's, she doesn't have time for anything else."

Alicia held out her hand, and Mark shook it. "Nice officially meeting you. I think we're going to see more of you around here."

Jason squinted, and Alicia grinned. He shook his head. "Come on back."

Mark followed as Jason pointed out an open area with four desks. Three displayed personal items and file folders, but the fourth was empty. Space for one more employee.

Jason waved a hand. "And there's our conference room."

A rectangular wooden table sat in the middle with eight rolling chairs around it. A window overlooked a small grassy area, a gravel alley and the back of another building.

Jason tapped a doorframe. "This is the office Shauna uses when she comes in to do the accounting." He stepped into the next doorway. "And this is my office." He took the seat behind his desk, and Mark sat in one of the two in front.

Mark leaned forward, elbows on his thighs. "I have a proposition. I'd like to join you here."

"You want to work for me?"

Mark snorted. For the entire time he and Jason had worked together, he'd been Jason's boss. "No. I want to buy into your business as half owner."

"You definitely would add to our skill set. You sure you want to give up traveling the world?"

Mark shook his head. "Seriously? For every resort or big city type of assignment, we had two in hellholes. Yeah, I can give that up. Especially since I'd be coming home to Kristy every night. Even Jack has given it up."

Jason leaned back and crossed his arms. "I don't really need an influx of cash."

"Do you have company owned cars?"

Jason shook his head. "We have expense accounts for mileage."

"It would be more professional if your employees drove clients in vehicles owned by the firm."

"Ward could sure use a company car. His must be at least ten years old. And Rico drives a Mini."

"See." Mark swept his arm around. "This is a great office and the location is perfect, but you're almost out of space. I think we should add a second floor, and move our offices up there, and add a second conference room. The investigators can stay down here."

"I'm renting the building." He grinned. "But I'm sure Dad would sell it to me. To us."

"I've got contacts, both for more employees and clients."

Jason stood. "Okay. You've sold me." He held out his

hand. "Partner."

Mark smiled and shook it. That was easier than expected. He'd had more points lined up, but that could wait for another time.

Mark sat back down. "Now, for the really important part. Shall we call this new venture *Simmons-Ballard Security and Investigations*? Our logo can include SBSI."

"I started it. Ballard should come first."

Mark grinned. "Do you want people to call it BS?"

Jason chuckled. "You do have a point. I'm going to enjoy working with you again."

Chapter 19

Kristy gripped Mark's hand as they entered the country club. The four of them had flown in late the night before, so she hadn't had a chance to stop by her father's. Now, she wouldn't be able to talk to him until after he was married.

They stopped beside a door with a paper labeled *Bride's Room*. Mark wrapped his arms around her and kissed her—all too briefly. She had to help Jessica get ready, and he had to get his best man suit on.

He kissed the tip of her nose. "You're going to rock your dress."

"As long as it's not pink or yellow, you know I will." Those were the only requirements she'd given Jess for her dress when she gave her measurements. She didn't know if it was long or short, full or body hugging. This day was for her dad and Jess. Although she hadn't done any of the planning, she'd do what she could to make everything else run perfectly.

Mark groaned. "Okay. I have to go find Jack." He gave her one last squeeze and took off.

Kristy opened the door and stepped in, closing it firmly behind her. Ah. There was her dress—a nice jade green. The bodice would hug her body and flow from there nearly to the floor. She turned at something being set on wood. Jessica stood in front of a vanity mirror, applying makeup.

"Jess!" Kristy hurried across the room and gave the bride a hug. The baby bump reminded her of the happy event scheduled a few months away. "You ready to get your dress on? Where is..." She spun around and found two wedding dresses hanging on hooks on the wall.

"Um. Jess. I never heard of a bride waiting until an hour before the wedding to choose which dress to wear."

Jess gave her a side hug and gripped her shoulder. "I picked mine out a couple of months ago. Yours is on the right."

"What?" On closer inspection, she realized it was the dress she'd fallen in love with when she and Shauna had gone shopping three weeks ago. Shauna had insisted they go to a bridal shop, and Kristy had been resistant at first. Once she'd tried on the first dress, she'd gotten into the spirit of it. She hadn't wanted the full skirted ones like Jessica's. Hers was fitted through the hips and flared to the floor. The top had embroidered leaves and vines the same white as the dress, spilling over to different lengths in the skirt. The top showed just the right amount of cleavage with a half-bare back and short cap sleeves. "How?" She pointed to the green dress. "But there's my bridesmaid dress."

The door opened and closed, and Kristy whirled around. Shauna stood by the door. "That would be for me."

Kristy flew across the room and hugged her friend. "I don't understand."

"We went bridal shopping because Mark asked me to take you. He gave me his credit card and said to get whatever dress you liked. While you were changing out of it, I was completing the sale for the dress and the shoes you'd tried on, and giving the saleswoman the address where to send it."

She hugged Shauna again. "Wow. That was so sweet how he made sure I picked out the dress I wanted." She turned to Jessica. "You're okay with this? We're crashing your wedding day."

She and Mark were getting married now rather than sometime later. And it was perfect that she and her dad would start their new lives on the same date.

Jess took Kristy's hands. "Jack asked me about it after Mark called. He thought it was a wonderful idea to share a wedding day with you, and I agree." She grinned. "And all the money saved from putting together a second wedding can go to the twins." She patted her tummy.

"You seem happy about having twins."

Jess did a cute folded-hands-under-her-chin thing. "I'm ecstatic. At almost forty, I'm getting into motherhood kind of late, so having two at once is perfect." For a couple of seconds her smile disappeared. "You should have seen me when I had to tell Jack I was pregnant. I mean, he's got a grown daughter"—she squeezed Kristy's arm—"and he's ten years older than me. I couldn't imagine he'd want to start over again."

Kristy grinned, already knowing how happy he was. He'd get to raise his children together with a wife who loved him as much as he loved her.

"After I blurted it out, he looked stunned for like five seconds, and I thought it was the end. Then he started laughing and scooped me up, spinning me in circles. It was like I'd given him Christmas, Halloween, and Easter all rolled into one." She dabbed her eyes. "And if I'm not careful, I'm going to ruin my makeup."

Kristy hugged her. "I'm so happy for you both."

Shauna clapped her hands. "Let's get going, ladies. We've got to move this along if we're going to make sure the wedding doesn't start without us."

They leaped into action, helping each other with dresses and hair. Kristy slipped on her shoes as a knock tapped on the door. A tall, brunette woman rushed in with three boxes.

"Sorry I'm late. A traffic accident had all the roads backed up." She sat the boxes on a table, opened the top one. "This is for the bridesmaid." She extracted a white rose bouquet with greenery and handed it to Shauna. "The brides have matching bouquets. This is the first time I've done flowers for a double wedding." She opened one box after the other, and lifted out the bouquets at the same time. Gorgeous. Red and white roses with greenery created bouquets a little larger than Shauna's, but not too large. She loved the combination.

The woman handed Kristy her flowers. She drew their beautiful scent into her lungs. They'd been so rushed getting ready that she hadn't had a chance to think. This was her wedding day. She'd come prepared to make this day special for her dad and Jessica, and they, along with Mark and Shauna were making it a special day for her, too.

"I think I'm in a dream."

Jess chuckled and gave her a one armed hug. "You and me, both. I'd be dead except for Jack."

Kristy's eyes widened. "I didn't know that."

"We'll have to tell you about it some time."

"Yeah, yeah," Shauna said. "We've got heroes for husbands, but they're playing our music."

Nerves struck Kristy. In a couple of minutes, she'd walk down the aisle towards Mark, towards a new life. She didn't know if she was ready for it. So much had changed in the last year. She'd changed. But for the better. And Mark was a big part of why. She straightened her shoulders. Nobody loved him as much as she did, and she would prove that to him every day.

The door opened, and the music grew louder. Shauna glanced back and smiled before disappearing to start her walk down the aisle.

Jessica grabbed Kristy's hand. "Do you want to go

together?"

"No. I think our dresses would be too crowded." Jess's had a full gathered skirt. "Besides, we intruded on your day. I want you to get undivided attention on your way down the aisle."

"Okay. I'm stopping beside my dad's seat for him to give me away. Then Jack will join me. You can come down the aisle then, and Jack will give you away."

"Sounds great. See you at the other end."

Kristy waited until the minister asked, "Who gives this woman to be wed?" and the response from Jess's father, then started her walk. Never in a million years did she think this would happen to her—have a wedding with a real wedding dress, and her man waiting for her.

She glanced at the end of the aisle and found Mark's gaze locked on her. There was her goal. Steps away from him, her father grabbed her arm and stopped her. Mark's grin widened. She was pretty sure he was trying not to laugh at her for forgetting to stop beside her dad.

Her father's arm wrapped around her, and he whispered in her ear. "I love you, honey, and I'm so glad we could share this day."

Tears pricked her eyes, but she wouldn't let them fall. "I love you, too, Dad. Thank you."

"Who gives this woman to be wed?" the minister asked.

Her dad hugged her closer. "I do."

Mark came down three steps and enclosed her hand in his, drawing her the rest of the way to the front. Her dad and Jessica joined them on the left. Kristy stood between the two men she loved. She couldn't ask for a better wedding.

"What about your family?" she whispered.

"They're here."

She was happy that he'd thought to share the special day with them. She wished she'd had a chance to meet them before the wedding.

They each said their vows, and Shauna handed her a ring to slide onto Mark's finger. It seemed he'd thought of everything. Hers was a perfect match for the engagement ring.

And the kiss. A wedding was the only time people didn't mind if a couple kissed in front of them. She was pretty sure Mark and her dad had a competition to see who could last the longest. At least to her, it felt like the longest wedding kiss she'd ever witnessed. Mark didn't stop until five seconds after the minister cleared his throat, and she was pretty sure her dad had poked him in the back with his elbow. At least, that's why she thought the crowd had laughed.

Mark lifted his head. "I love you. Forever."

"Forever." She couldn't resist giving him another quick kiss.

***

Mark closed the hotel room door. "You rocked your dress, but I need to get you out of it."

All afternoon and evening, he'd watched her, danced with her, kissed her, and the thought that kept coming back was that he wanted to peel her dress off. The front showed off just enough cleavage for him to want to see the rest. Her back was exposed low enough she couldn't have worn a bra, and every time he danced with her or kissed her, he ran his hands over it. The dress hugged her hips then flared out in a full skirt.

Her hands overlapped on the back of his neck. "Did you see it before the wedding?"

He worked the zipper down. "No. You took my breath away as you marched towards me down the aisle." He kissed her cheek. If his lips touched hers, he'd be lost too soon. Too many kisses at the reception had him craving all of her.

He chuckled. "I loved how you forgot you were supposed to stop beside your dad." Their gazes had locked, and the world had disappeared for her as much as for him.

He pushed the dress straps off her shoulders.

Kristy lowered her arms and the garment slid into a foot-tall heap surrounding her. She stepped out of it and laid the dress across a chair. "It's too bad a wedding dress is only worn for a few hours. It seems like such a waste of money. If I'd known I was picking my actual dress, I would have checked price tags."

He kissed her and backed her against the wall, pressing her now bare breasts against his chest. He wore too many layers and would have to remedy that soon. "That dress was beautiful on you. I'm glad you didn't check prices. Shauna said you two had fun."

"We did, and I didn't suspect a thing." She unbuttoned his shirt. He'd stuck his tie in his coat pocket hours ago. Kristy pushed the shirt off his shoulders, and it fell to the floor with his jacket. "A t-shirt, too? Weren't you hot?"

He chuckled at her disappointment and tugged the shirt over his head. "Only when I had you in my arms."

He couldn't take anymore. He had a special night planned for the first time with his wife. The three weeks since he'd put the wedding plan into motion, it'd taken a lot of acting to not drop any hints.

He stripped off his shoes and the rest of his clothes. Moments later, her shoes and panties were gone, too. He swept her up and carried her to bed but set her down beside it to tear back the covers. They got into bed, and he gathered her tight against him, sliding a leg between hers. He'd never get tired of the way her body made him sizzle and become ultra sensitive to every touch.

He kissed her, but she leaned her head back into the pillow. "Wait. I have to tell you something."

He nibbled her lip. "That you love me, and you're glad we got married today?"

"Um. Okay. Yes, and—"

He nibbled her lip again. "And you're pregnant."

She slapped his shoulder. "Hey. That was my news. How did you know?"

He chuckled and kissed her. "Because we've made love every day since I got you back. And no periods."

"Oh. Well, this is the first time I haven't been on birth control, so I didn't know if my cycle might be longer than normal. Some women's are. I didn't take a pregnancy test until three days ago."

He kissed her jaw and worked his way to her ear. "And you didn't tell me then."

"With Dad's wedding so close, I figured I'd tell you now. After the wedding. So, ta-da. I'm pregnant."

"All right. Apology accepted."

"What?"

He leaned back and met her gaze. "Next time, I want to be there when you take the pregnancy test."

Her eyebrows rose. "You want to watch me pee on a stick?"

He grinned. "You can do that in private, but I want to hold you while we wait for the results."

"I was on pins and needles doing it. I wish I'd done it with you. I'm sorry."

He covered her flat stomach. "I want to go with you to some of your appointments. I want to hear our baby's heartbeat. I want to see our baby on the ultrasound."

She wrapped her arms around his neck. "Me, too. I want to share it all with you. And if I have morning sickness, I'm sharing that, too."

He laughed. "You're too cute."

"I'll be too frustrated if my husband doesn't make love to me now."

"We don't want that." Mark had loved Kristy the first time they'd been together, but that paled compared to the way he loved her now. "I need to tell you something, too."

She pouted. "This better be worth delaying my orgasm."

Yeah. It was. "We're going back to *Pirates' Cove* for our honeymoon."

She vaulted up and rolled him onto his back. "We are? Let me show you how much I love you."

It would be hard to top their first time as husband and wife on the honeymoon.

***

Kristy punched the doorbell but couldn't resist another kiss before her dad answered the door. She grabbed Mark's neck and pulled him down, planting one on him.

He chuckled. "You remember we did this in the car"—he pointed behind him—"right there on the street."

"I know. But you're my husband. It still seems surreal, and I need to make sure you're here."

The door opened. "Kristy. Mark, come on in." Her dad stepped back, and she gave him a hug when she passed.

As soon as her mom died, he'd sold their house and moved into an apartment. He and Jessica had picked out this house together, and Kristy hadn't seen it yet.

"Come on through. We're having lunch on the screened porch."

Kristy followed her dad through the kitchen. He opened a French door and stepped down into the sunny room. A table was set with four place settings and covered dishes in the center.

Jessica sat on a wicker couch at the other end of the porch. She set down her paperback, greeted Kristy with a hug, then squeezed Mark's hand. "So nice to see you two without the rush and crush." She gestured to the table. "Lunch is ready, so let's sit down."

They filled their plates. "Dad, I don't think I heard where you two are going on your honeymoon."

"It's on a Caribbean island."

Kristy's gaped at Mark. He wiped his mouth with a napkin, but she knew he was covering a laugh. She loved her dad but didn't want to share the same resort for their honeymoons.

"Oh. Which one?"

"It's on St. Martin."

Her shoulders relaxed. They might be in the same part of the ocean, but it wasn't the same island.

Kristy touched Mark's leg under the table, and he clasped her hand. "While you're getting used to being a dad to little ones again, you'll have to get used to being called Grandpa."

He grinned. "That was some wedding night."

"Dad! At least we were engaged when I got pregnant."

"Touché. It's too bad you're not going to live around here. Our little ones could play with their niece or nephew."

She squeezed her dad's hand. "I know. I'm kind of torn about that. We'll have to make frequent visits. And the house we're maybe getting"—she crossed her fingers—"has room for house guests." They'd put an offer in the morning before they left but hadn't had a response yet.

With the meal finished, her dad stood. "Kristy, I'd like to talk to you privately for a few minutes."

She gave a side glance to Mark, and he shrugged, not seeming to know what it was about. She didn't have a clue what he needed to talk about that couldn't include Mark and Jessica.

"Um. Sure." She followed him into the house and sat on the couch in the living room.

He took her hands. "I want to apologize. For not being a better father."

"What? You were the best father ever. I have really great memories of all the fun things we did together."

"I was trying to make up for those times I couldn't be there. I thought we had a good arrangement, your mother taking care of you when I wasn't there."

"Your marriage was an arrangement?"

He rubbed the back of his head. "Not from the beginning. We got married too young, and we weren't who we thought we were. She needed a husband who was always there for her. I didn't see that because she was so loving and doting when I was home." He shook his head. "I think you'd just started high school when I stumbled upon irrefutable evidence she was cheating. I couldn't believe how blind I was. She agreed to keep her affairs quiet, but since I'd found out, I don't think she cared anymore."

All that time when she tried to protect him, they could have at least commiserated together. She swiped a tear off her cheek.

"Honey, I'm so sorry. I realized when you were finishing high school, and your, ah, commitment issues, that your mother damaged you. I didn't know what I could do to change it by then. I should have quit the service or not gone into private security. I should have found a nine-to-five job and divorced her. Taken custody of you. I trusted too much in a mother's love."

She threw herself into his arms. "I tried to protect you by not telling you about her affairs. I thought you loved her so much, and I didn't want you to get hurt." She sat back.

"I know it's no consolation for you, but I quit the security company. I'm teaching."

She giggled. "Are you teaching subterfuge?"

"Something like that. Anyway, I'll be a big part of these babies' lives."

"I'm glad for them. You'll be the best father ever."

The doorbell rang, and he glanced towards the door. "That visitor is for you. Why don't you go freshen up, and I'll let them in."

She narrowed her eyes.

The bell rang again. "Go on."

She made a guess where the bathroom was and found it. She had no idea who'd be calling here for her. Kristy stared at her makeup. It could do with a bit of repair, but she didn't have her purse. She patted under her eyes with a tissue. It would be fine.

She bit her lip. What would her life have been like if she'd told her dad what was happening? For sure, if he'd found out what that one boyfriend of her mother's had done with her, he would have taken her away from her mother. She'd probably have gone to a therapist then and maybe had a totally different high school experience.

She sighed. Water under the bridge. She couldn't go back and change it.

Shoulders back, she was ready to face whatever guest her father had invited.

Voices drew her to the living room. Mark and Jessica had joined her dad and the mysterious guest. She stopped beside Mark, and he put an arm around her.

The guest was a man a bit older than her father—gray at the temples of his otherwise black hair. Wrinkles around his eyes hinted at a lot of time spent outdoors. Even in a suit, he had a military bearing.

Her father broke the silence that had dropped at her return. "Kristy, I'd like you to meet Major Saunders. Major, this is my daughter, Kristy Simmons."

She nearly giggled but kept a straight face. Barely. Being introduced for the first time with her new name took precedence over the major. "Nice meeting you, Major." She squinted at her father.

"Major," her dad said, "perhaps you can explain why I invited you."

"It's come to our attention that you have encryption skills that would be an asset." He slanted a glance at her dad. "I hear you can decode anything put in front of you. In fact, I recently found out you unwittingly decoded a couple of messages for us."

Her breath caught in her lungs. She glanced at her father. Deep breath. Let it out. "Dad? When did this happen?" When she was about eight, they'd started the encryption puzzles. She called it spy games, so he'd make the solutions sound like captured information.

"Twice when you were sixteen, a couple of months apart. We had the best people working on them, and after three days, they hadn't cracked the codes. We were desperate for the information, so I took a chance. You had them solved in a couple of hours. You saved lives and didn't even know it."

"Wow." She'd saved lives. The past few weeks, people died because of her skills. It helped balance it out.

Her dad clasped her hand. "I took credit since I didn't want anyone to know I'd given sensitive information to a civilian teenager. But I was so proud of you." He dropped her hand.

"Which brings me to my visit," Major Saunders said. "We'd like you to join our intelligence gathering team. You'd be an important asset as a cryptographer."

"Seriously? How did this come up now?"

The major glanced at her dad. "Your father suggested it."

He'd known forever what she could do. "Mark asked me to find out where your skills might fit in. I thought decrypting was only a hobby. I should have asked you."

Communication between them had been sorely missing. She stared at her husband and his adoring face. "I can't believe you did this for me."

"I'm just a middleman here. But I knew how much you loved it. And you're good at it. And I know you can stick to this better than all those other jobs that bored you." He smirked.

She would not kiss Mark in front of the major. She would not... She kissed his jaw.

She studied the major's face. "I just got married, and we're settling into our new hometown. I don't want to—"

"You'll be working remotely. We'll set you up with a secure laptop, and you'll only have to come in a couple days every month or two." He handed her a card. "Here's the address."

She glanced at her father. "Dad, is this your old building?"

"Yes, it is."

It sounded perfect. She didn't think she could get paid for doing something she loved. And she could visit her dad when she went into the office. She grinned at Mark.

His eyes crinkled as if he was smiling, but his lips suppressed it. "It's your decision, baby."

She faced Major Saunders and held out her hand. "You've got yourself a new employee, Major."

He shook her hand and lifted his briefcase from where it leaned against his leg. "Unfortunately, we've got a packet of paperwork to fill out, with non-disclosures and so forth. There's one for security clearance, but Jack assures me you'll pass with no problem." He glanced at her dad. "Jack, kitchen table?"

Her dad pointed. "Dining room is through there."

She followed him, and he pointed to a wooden chair. "Have a seat." He extracted a stack of papers and two pens from his case. With one pen he pointed to a figure. "That's your starting yearly pay."

Kristy clamped a hand over her mouth so she wouldn't squeal. The pay was three times the amount of her best paying job.

He pointed below the number. "After six months, you'll be evaluated, and if you're as good as Jack says you are, you'll get a substantial raise." He tapped the number again. "Initial here."

Kristy added her new initials to the page.

"Read the rest and sign the bottom of each page."

And so it began. Thirty minutes later, she had a job with…she didn't even know which branch of the government.

He handed her a card. "I know you're leaving for your honeymoon in a couple days. Once you're back, come to the address on the card to pick up your laptop. It can't be shipped. Plan on being there about three hours."

She walked him to the door. "Thank you, Major, for this chance. You won't regret it."

"See you in a couple of weeks, Kristy."

She closed the door and raced to the living room. Mark stood and slid one foot back to catch her weight. She threw herself at him, and he caught her. She put all her excitement into a kiss.

She dropped her head to his shoulder. "I can't believe how much they're paying me to have fun."

He ran his hand down her back. "They're paying you to do something not many people can do."

She placed her hands on each side of his face. "Thank you for thinking of it. Oh. We'll have to change our flight back. I have to pick up the laptop after our honeymoon."

"Not a problem." His phone rang, and he glanced at the screen. "It's the realtor."

Kristy laced her fingers and tightened them until her knuckles turned white.

"Mark Simmons."

Kristy waited while he gave monosyllabic responses. Finally, her heart soared with the words she wanted to hear.

"Accept their counter-offer and email me the contract."

Kristy squealed, and he grinned. Her whole world had fallen into place. From non-relationships to a husband who loved her as much as she loved him. A baby on the way. The best job ever. And now a house four blocks from Shauna's. Oh, yeah. And a honeymoon that would put to shame the first time they'd been to *Pirates' Cove*.

Mark pocketed his phone and wrapped his arms around her. "Are you happy, baby?"

She stared into his eyes. "I am so, so happy. But you need to know that if it was just you and me in a shack somewhere…Okay, it would have to be a clean, warm shack. But anyway, just the two of us there, I would still be happy."

He touched his pocket. "Do you want me to call the realtor back?"

She laughed. "I'm going to enjoy spending the next hundred years with you."

THE END

214

The next book in the series – *Tony's to Protect*

When his instant family is targeted by evil, he'll use all his skills to keep them safe.

Life was tough when Bryanna's boyfriend died, leaving her two months pregnant. She left Boston and moved to the small town of Rawlins where things are a little strange. Some residents are like her and have special powers. It's the perfect place to raise her twin daughters who likely have powers too.

Tony Ballard grew up in Rawlins, knows many of its secrets, and has a few of his own. When he saves a toddler with his abilities, he meets the woman of his dreams, literally. Bryanna starred in his way-too-sexy dreams, and he realizes the dreams were premonitions.

Family isn't always welcome. Bryanna's kids' great-aunt arrives in town. The woman has wicked plans for the girls, but not if Tony has anything to say about it. He will do anything to protect the woman he's fallen in love with and her daughters.

Books by Deborah Wallace

Rawlins Series (Paranormal Romance – witches)
Kathleen's Legacy
Jason's Forbidden Woman
Jamie's Trials
Adam's Redemption
Kristy's Puzzle
Tony's to Protect
Abby's Salem Legacy – *Fall 2023*

Wounded Warrior Hearts Series (Clean Romance)
Wounded Warrior Hearts: Steven
Wounded Warrior Hearts: Amy
Wounded Warrior Hearts: Russ

Choice Series (Romantic Suspense)
Second Choice
Third Choice
No Choice
Her Choice
Series Complete

Unknown Series (Romantic Suspense)
Father Unknown
Killer Unknown
Series complete

Other Books (Romantic Suspense)
I Shot the Sheriff
Your Love Belongs to Me
Summer Love
Searching for Stephanie

New Memories – Receive this book free by signing up for my newsletter. https://dl.bookfunnel.com/jioszdyc5a

Check out my website for details on these books and where to find them. You can also sign up to receive emails when I have a new book. www.DeborahWallaceBooks.com.

You can find my books on my Amazon author page. amazon.com/author/deborahwallacebooks

I would love if you left a review of my book on your favorite Book sites. Thank you.

About Deborah Wallace

Someone suggested I try writing, and stories started populating my brain, begging to be put on paper (or my computer screen).

I've got quite a number of books under my belt, but the ones I keep coming back to are the romantic suspense. When I wrote the first *Rawlins* book, I thought it would be the only paranormal. Then I said 'what if…' and now children of the first characters and a couple of friends have books.

I have been called a Jane-of-all-trades, from seamstress to house and furniture designer/builder to computer programmer to technical writer and bookkeeper. I even do car maintenance. I've also guided a team of 'Future Problem Solvers'.

I grew up in Michigan, but Massachusetts has been my home for more years than I care to think about. I love the history here, the museums and antique houses, the seacoast and hiking trails.

My three children have grown and scattered, but my husband is by my side, encouraging my writing.